"Pritchard possesses a gift for depicting diverse characters, times and locales. . . . Only through self-analysis, and undergoing a jolting experience, do these women, and men, transcend their pain."   —*Ms.*

"Melissa Pritchard is one of our finest writers."
—Annie Dillard,
author of *Pilgrim At Tinker Creek*

"Pritchard's meticulously crafted prose bursts at its own seams with inventiveness."
—*The Harvard Review*

"Impressive. . . . With each story the collection gains momentum. . . . Pritchard's prose is spare and wrenching."   —*Publishers Weekly*

"[Pritchard's] writing . . . is beautiful, graphic, aggressive—and always smart."
—*The Bloomsbury Review*

"Stories, like their heroine, so brave and full of life."   —*Kirkus Reviews*

MELISSA PRITCHARD

Disappearing Ingenue

Melissa Pritchard is the author of two short story collections, *The Instinct for Bliss* and *Spirit Seizures,* and two novels, *Phoenix* and *Selene of the Spirits.* Pritchard was awarded a Pushcart Prize for "Funktionslust," which appeared in *The Paris Review.* Her story "Salve Regina" was included in *Prize Stories 2000: The O. Henry Awards.* Among numerous other awards, she has received the Flannery O'Connor Award, the Janet Heidinger Kafka Prize, and a Howard Foundation Fellowship from Brown University. She is Director of the M.F.A. Creative Writing Program at Arizona State University and is on the faculty of Spalding University.

Disappearing Ingenue

STORIES

MELISSA PRITCHARD

Anchor Books

A Division of Random House, Inc.

New York

These stories have appeared, sometimes in slightly different form, in the following publications: "Her Last Man," *The American Voice,* No. 45, Spring 1998; "Port de Bras," *The Southern Review,* Vol. 34, No. 2, Spring 1998 (cited in *1999 Best American Short Stories, The Pushcart Prize, Prize Stories 1999: The O. Henry Awards*); "Salve Regina," *The Gettysburg Review,* April 1999, and *Prize Stories 2000: The O. Henry Awards,* editor Larry Dark, Random House, October 2000; "The Widow's Poet," *Boulevard,* Vol. 15, No. 3, Spring 2000; "Funktionslust," *The Paris Review,* No. 153, Winter 1999-2000, and *The Pushcart Prize XXVI,* editor Bill Henderson, November 2001; "The Case of the Disappearing Ingenue," *Dark Horse Literary Review,* Vol. 1, No. 1, Spring 2000; "High Fidelity," *Alligator Juniper,* Prescott College, Prescott, AZ, 2000; "Virgin Blue," *Open City,* No. 11, Summer/Fall 2000.

"Won't You Be My Neighbor" © Fred Rogers. Used with permission from Fred M. Rogers and Family Communications, Inc.

The Library of Congress has cataloged the Doubleday edition as follows:
Pritchard, Melissa.
Disappearing Ingenue : the misadventures of Eleanor Stoddard / by Melissa Pritchard.—1st ed.
p. cm.
1. Women—Fiction. I. Title.
PS3566.R578 D57 2002
813'.54—dc21 2001052737

Anchor ISBN: 0-385-72189-7

Author photograph © Roni Ziemba
Book design by Gretchen Achilles

www.anchorbooks.com

Printed in the United States of America
10 9 8 7 6 5 4 3 2 1

TO THE MEMORY

OF

ROBERT GARY ROMANISKY

1949–1970

AND

SISTER MARGARET "MARNIE" WALKER DILLING, R.S.C.J.

1940–1997

Acknowledgments

I would like to thank the George A. and Eliza Gardner Howard Foundation Fellowship in Creative Writing from Brown University as well as the Women's Studies Department at Arizona State University for invaluable financial assistance. For his brilliant and sustaining friendship, I am grateful to Michael Murphy. I am particularly indebted to women friends and associates who have supported and believed in me during the writing of these stories—Florence Forrest, Deneen Jenks, Diane Williams, Deborah Ackerman, Laura Tohe, Lori Voepel, Susan McCabe, Susannah Meadows, Grace McKeaney, Mary Clyde, Toi Derricotte, Elizabeth Gaffney, Sallie Bingham, Allyson Stack, Joyce Carol Oates, Sena Jeter Naslund, Jillian Robinson, Colette Korry Hatrick, Pamela Painter, Pinna Joseph, Alicia Erian, Valerie Jeremijenko, Kristina McGrath, Marianne Moloney, Eugenia Sutcliffe, Lynda Seefeldt, my mother, Helen Reilly Brown, my sister Penelope Byrd, my daughters Noelle and Caitlin, my superb agent, Joy Harris, and most excellent editor, Deborah Futter—these women, courageous, intelligent, and lovely beyond telling, have my heart.

Rightly, in every age, it is assumed we are witnessing the disappearance of the last traces of paradise.

E. M. CIORAN

A woman can look both moral and exciting—if she also looks as if it were quite a struggle.

EDNA FERBER

Contents

Disappearing Ingenue

Port de Bras

(PORT D' BRAH). PORT: CARRY. BRAS: ARMS.

ANY CARRYING, OR MOVEMENT, OF THE ARMS.

Ballerina is a magic word. Any girl who hears it pictures in her mind a beautiful dancer in a sparkling costume, skimming along on the tips of her toes, seeming to fly like a bird. Of course, the dancer in the girl's imagination usually turns out to be herself.

—MAE BLACKER FREEMAN

Fun with Ballet: A Beginner's Book for Future Ballerinas

I first met Donna Rae Earps while suspended upside down by my knees. She hung beside me, the new girl from Livermore, not caring if her white tulle petticoat rocked over her head like a motel lampshade or that the elastic waistband on her panties was shot six ways to Sunday, as my mother would surely have said. With her single braid like a flat gold belt snapping the dirt, her narrow, piquant face going redder by the second, nothing was more obvious to me than our destined friendship and nothing less clear than its surprising end.

There had been, during our sixth grade's last two weeks of school, a spotty epidemic of witless but irresistible Chinaman jokes. So when, with some small difficulty due to my weight, I spun off the steel bar and landed upright in the school yard, I showed the new girl what Kristine Leipzig had pointed out to me that morning: a Chinaman's face staring straight up from my left kneecap. When she asked, I examined Donna Rae's kneecaps—they were smooth and white, unblemished—but didn't see anybody.

"Who'd you put there if you could?" I was panting, another excuse my mother had for enrolling me in Miss Gita's Academy of Ballet. Besides "acquiring a feminine carriage," I was supposed to get "toned":

"My baby brother." Her face, still radishy, looked tragic and closed. "Or my mother. She's dead, too."

I told myself, by way of both consolation and awe, that Donna Rae Earps was pageant-beautiful. At twelve, she was a thoroughbred of physicality, lily amid the weeds, jewel among rough stones. Whereas I, Eleanor Stoddard, the most worried person I knew, seemed cut out to be a politician, a circuit court judge or an FBI detective like Fred Borcher's brother-in-law. Fred Borcher owned the local butcher shop, and my mother bought meat from him, my father liked to tease, just so they could chew the fat, sling dirt on people they had both known too long, since high school in fact. As for me, whatever demanded a qualmish and squinted view of the world, that's what I seemed headed for. (Though who I yearned to be, since Miss Lassiter made us read her diary, was Anne Frank. A heroine, suffering tedious roommates and vicious enemies, smarter and quicker than the adults around her. I learned enough, that summer of 1960, to respect my worry and to understand there were legitimate reasons to fret. I read and reread *The Diary of Anne Frank,* lay awake plotting the circumstance that would empty me out.)

So while Donna Rae was all sinewy catlike grace, I was inclined to sit and be one of two things, a staring or a reading lump. Which is how we wound up at the *barre* together in Miss Gita's Academy of Ballet, I to be toned, blah, blah, and Donna Rae to *plié* (plee-AY), *demi-plié* (d'mee plee-AY), *pas de chat* (pas d'SHAH) and tuck in her spoon-sized *derrière* (dare ee AIR) with cool aplomb.

FROM HER FIRST LESSON, Donna Rae took to the ballerina regime as impeccably as I managed to insult it. Her bedroom became her studio, and while she *relevéd* (re-levAYED) on pink satin toe shoes she wasn't even supposed to have yet, but that she'd talked Mr. Earps, who didn't know a thing about ballet except what she told him, into buying, I'd flop across her pink canopy bed, asking myself whether I would have had Anne's courage, locked in a secret annex in Amsterdam. Moreover, how would I know unless I devised trials of character, secret hurdles of courage—a virtue, I decided, that could only be incrementally acquired. I fasted, stuck bits of colored fish-gravel in my shoes, held my breath until my lungs burned, pierced the skin of each of my fingertips with sterilized needles. I kept a secret list of these things, for what I wanted, eventually, was to shine in moral crisis. I even chopped my hair, that hateful bramble of dust, to look more like Anne's. One afternoon, Donna Rae, who knew nothing of my list or my ambition, thumbtacked white bedsheets over her curtainless windows, switched off the overhead light, lit a circle of twelve white candles, and danced inside her arena of flames. She insisted I take the boy's part, catching her as she *jetéd* (jeh-TAYED) off a small yellow kitchen chair. Later, I helped her write ballet definitions and pronunciations on pieces of paper that she taped to her walls. *Arabesque* (ar a BESK), *barre* (bar), *battement tendu* (baht MAW tawn DU), *frappé* (frah PAY), *pas de bourrée* (pah d'borr AY), *sur les pointes* (soor lay pawnt), on and on; they would make dry, fluttering sounds as she leapt and pirouetted (peer-oh-WETTED) around her room.

Some part of her grace came from having to dance noiselessly so as not to wake her father, asleep in the next room. I had seen Ray Earps awake once, standing in front of an open refrigerator, and he had looked like an Everly Brother whom fame had not yet reached, or worse, had bypassed. He worked at the same place my father did, Stanford Research Institute; Ray worked nights cleaning and maintaining the computers my dad designed. "Fried-egg sandwich," he'd grinned, saluting me with a blackened spatula, an egg hanging lifelessly over its sides. He'd worn a blue shirt with a pack of cigarettes shoved into each rolled-up sleeve. His hair was a darker blond than Donna Rae's, and it languished in a wide, sensuous curl down his forehead and feathered into a ducktail at the back. I knew his wife had been the drama instructor at Livermore High before she'd died in the same car wreck as the baby brother. Donna Rae showed me the photograph she kept beneath her pillow.

"You don't have a picture of him, too?" I felt inexplicably jealous.

"That's his fire truck." She gestured airily to a toy engine high on an otherwise empty shelf. "I'm never supposed to touch it."

So, I decided, the tragic deaths of his wife and son accounted for the overstuffed pale blue wing chair on the front porch, the granulated hill of silver beer cans, the sampler-sized whiskey bottles stubbed like wet fruit into the leafless hedge beneath the picture window. Ornaments of sorrow. I listened for Ray Earps sleeping on the other side of the wall. I made no noise as I lay on the canopy bed, listening to Donna Rae hum what sounded like Ferrante and Teicher's "Theme from *Exodus*" while she worked her way through *demi-pliés, grand pliés* and *arabesques* with a joy in her own movement that struck me as foreign and nearly unbearable.

The one time I got to invite Donna Rae over for dinner, my mother said afterward that she didn't trust her. That was the word she used, "trust." She said her clothes looked cheap and badly laundered, her table manners were poor . . . (*The Goops they lick their fingers, and the Goops they lick their knives; They spill their broth on the tablecloth, oh, they lead disgusting lives!*) . . , her father *was* obviously a blue-collar type, and even if he *was* working to put food on the table, it wouldn't do, leaving a twelve-year-old alone at night. Donna Rae seemed to know my mother didn't like her, seemed used to being distrusted, and never again asked to come to my house. So late Wednesday afternoons, we'd meet at the corner of Cortez and Balboa—the streets in our neighborhood were all named for Spanish explorers—and swinging our round plastic ballet cases, we'd walk the six blocks to Miss Gita's Academy. The ballet school was inside a Spanish-style bungalow, a house converted to office space, and was protected by a yellowish-green fortress of stately, peeling eucalyptus trees. Sometimes, when the piano music stopped, we would hear typing coming through one of the walls or a telephone shrilling in the real estate office next door.

Miss Florence Gita's constant companion and authority was a slender black stick she struck against the floor or whacked dryly against her long, flat palm as we rallied to keep time. Each week she appeared in a royal-blue, long-sleeved leotard, her wandlike legs in snowy tights, her narrow feet encased in glossy, black slippers that reminded me of giant éclairs. A short white chiffon skirt was bolted to her waist, and her strangely marbled blond-and-gray hair—shaped into the most extraordinary bun, large as a second head—hung like some awful, wilting flower from the nape of her rigidly fluted neck. Her *derrière* was flat as a shirt box, her hips winged out like a cow's; her whole image was shocking to me, and I cannot say why.

Miss Gita detested me, and—stung by the unfairness—I detested her back. To her I must have been a living war on beauty, there by way of my mother's dream of rehabilitation: a sullen, wild-haired lummox in twisted, linty black tights, with a *derrière* like a brick. I also had insanely high arches. At least once a class, I would drop to the floor in the midst of an ensemble exercise, whinnying with pain, gripping whichever arch had collapsed this time, my pear shape mocked in three sets of wall mirrors. I was only partially absolved by being Donna Rae's friend, and tried to hide behind her gamine shape and passionate clean attention. A dozen times during class, Miss Gita would single her out: "Open your eyes girls, the classic *pas de chat,*" "the perfect *glissade,*" on and on. Donna Rae made us all look stilty and bad, an especially embittering experience for Hayley Schmadabeck, once the Mosquito's pet, now demoted to a second-rate resin-collector like the rest of us.

I COULDN'T EXACTLY ASK did they die right away, so I said, "What was his name? Your brother's?"

We were playing Ping-Pong under the walnut tree in my backyard, a game I played with torpid motions of the wrist or slothful extensions of the arm, my strategy was to make the ball come to me, the single, stolid force it could not avoid. Tapping the hollow white sphere, I repeated my question. Donna Rae, her hair stacked up in a "Grace Kelly coronet" (exactly what she called it), answered as she clipped the ball back, and I missed it.

"Roland Arnold Earps. His initials turn into the same name as me and my dad."

I was now prowling in the long grass beneath the table, hoping not to be bitten by earwigs. Her voice filtered dreamily down.

"Roland died on the morning of his fourth birthday. He and my mom were driving his birthday cake back to the bakery my aunt owned—we always got our cakes for free. The design on top was supposed to be a fire engine, but when we opened the box it was a cowboy-shaped cake with the name Billy Swan and the number eight written like a lasso."

I reemerged to spank the ball off the table's left edge, my one trick.

"They got killed because somebody at Aunt Dora's bakery got two boys' cakes confused. My dad'll never get over it. Oh, cripes . . ." Donna Rae had just lofted the ball, like some light, blown egg, over our new fence and into the Murphys' yard. At my mother's insistence, my father had recently erected the woven redwood fence to better seal the Murphys' lives off from ours.

"Our entire dining room was decorated with little yellow

ladders and red fire helmets. The ceiling was hung with red and yellow streamers with a fan blowing up to look like flames. My dad refused to let anyone touch any of it. How do we get the ball back?"

If her skipping from one thing to another like that seemed shallow, still, no one I knew besides Doc Hargreaves had died, so what, really, did I know? Since I was born, Doc had been our neighbor—a bald, avuncular, onion-headed man who wore, year-round, a smelly tweed fedora and a poisonous-colored sport coat in the pockets of which were wrapped hard candies you had to work to pick the lint off of. He spoke in plain rhyme—*What's the story, morning glory? Where's the shoe, cock-ledoo?*—and if it didn't rhyme, he didn't say it. When he died (of family neglect, my mother said) his small green stucco house was immediately sold to the Murphys. This distressed my mother, yet she did the neighborly thing and, the day they moved in, carried over a lemon cake and a chipped-beef casserole. She returned, minutes later, appalled. *Beat-all-Catholics,* she hissed, not sounding like my mother at all. *Living like pigs. Dumber than stumps.* She forbade me to play with any of the five children, which thrust an unearned sense of superiority upon me, yet also forged curiosity. What was their offense? What was wrong with Catholics? In our house no one said grace or gave thanks. My father dropped me off at a nearby Episcopal church on Sundays at nine and picked me up one hour later, no questions asked. Hard work, cleanliness, thrift—these formed our creed. No one raised the sorts of schmoozy, profligate questions that led to a need for theology in the first place. In fact, as the Ping-Pong ball zinged over the fence, I remembered it was Sunday, and the nearest we came to practicing religion in our house was the pork roast and apple pie we ate every Sunday night, a dinner to which Donna Rae would never be invited. "There's a way in through the alley," I said.

We prodded around in weeds and nettles and trash, hunted among dozens of volunteer maple saplings that had formed a dense miniature forest, and ended up, without our Ping-Pong ball, beside the mint-green stucco house. The Murphys' dented brown sedan was gone from the driveway, leaving behind a long, oily splotch. It was unusually silent, so I figured the Murphys were at noon Mass. We crept to a window and peered in, and what we saw drove us to the next window and the next. The wild disorder I saw in the hallway, in the kitchen, was repeated in every room—a squalor like I had never seen, a mess that enthralled me. Donna Rae saw Mrs. Murphy first. She was sitting up in bed, her hands steepled on her mountainous belly. I thought she looked sad and martyred. She was also doing nothing, a concept foreign at my house.

"Ish. She looks like a pillbug." I followed Donna Rae who had boldly unlatched the chain-link front gate and was now glissading sideways down the street, her arms raised in a port de bras, explaining what Mr. Murphy had done to Mrs. Murphy to make her have to sit without moving until the baby was born. "Six fucks, six kids."

"What?"

"It's called fucking, and it's a bad word. Don't say it. Swear."

I swore, and later, as Donna Rae leapt, faunlike, inside her white grove of candles, I lay faceup on the bed, hostage to a vaguely thrilling scenario of Mr. Murphy whating Mrs. Murphy, and, beside them, the five little whated-into-existence Murphys strung like natural rosary beads, backs turned, sucking on pruny, bitter thumbs.

I AGREED TO MEET Donna Rae outside the Burlingame public library at noon. Having withstood the librarian's flinty glance of disapproval, I now sat on a stone bench, feeling the moral weight of seven Holocaust books on my lap. Books were paths that led away from and back to myself; they were self-selective, uncannily autobiographical. The previous summer I had read everything on ghosts, poltergeists, possessions and hauntings; the summer before had been horses, *Misty of Chincoteague,* etcetera. Now it was the Holocaust, and I had just been made to feel ashamed of my curiosity.

We had disagreed over what Miss Gita's house would look like, and when Donna Rae finally showed up and we walked the block and a half to the address inked on her wrist, my prediction turned out to be the more accurate. Miss Gita lived inside a square, pencil-yellow house with blank, white metal awnings. Neat but ugly. Clean but ominous. Nothing grew. There were even two plots of dark green gravel instead of grass.

I pointed to the sharklike gray fins of an old Cadillac sticking out from behind the house.

"Go knock." I was crabby because my arms were tired, because it was the hottest part of the day, because the house was so hideous.

Donna Rae made it up three of four cement steps before she turned and flitted back to the sidewalk.

"What?"

"I think when you visit, you're supposed to bring a little gift." Little gift? That sounded like a mother talking, but I couldn't say that. After all.

As Donna Rae, spurred by disappointment, hurtled through a round of *pas de chat, pas de bourrée* and a vertiginous series of pirouettes, I worried that either her long-flying hair or her leotard might catch fire. I also told her my mother had refused to let me walk down to Broadway until she realized the dog was out of food; so if I stopped at Fred Borcher's, I could go. George was a dark red bratwurst, a "dashhound," a dachshund, a Rhineland wiener dog. He was twelve, like me, though in dog years that translated into the news that he should be dead. Pink epilepsy pills spiked his specialty food, and his water intake had to be rationed because of incontinence. My mother spoiled George, talking to him in a pippy baby-voice he loved. My fun came from plugging him under a sisal wastebasket in our back-yard and watching it twirl frenziedly around the lawn and carom into the trunks of trees.

For what must have been the fortieth time, I studied the photograph of June Earps. With her pixie haircut and round, sad eyes, she made me think of a depressed elf.

"How come there's no picture of your brother?"

I was convinced Donna Rae did not possess the same flesh and bones I did. Dropping into a deep, willowy back-bend, she turned slightly, staring dramatically through glossy streams of hair. Though I suppose I loved watching her, I resented being her constant audience.

"People said, except for our age, we could have been twins. We looked exactly alike. Did you bring your money?"

I nodded, having in fact filched five of the newer and less valuable coins from my silver dollar collection, a theft I would record on my secret list and later erase.

BROADWAY, BURLINGAME, WAS one long, supple road of neigh-borly commerce. It began with a sign at the intersection of El Camino Real and Broadway—a wide, licorice-black arch bridg-ing the street, the letters BROADWAY whitely marching across. It ended five or so blocks later at the train station where com-muters made the forty-five-minute trip north to San Francisco.

My mother had gone to Our Lady of Angels High School with Lou Giotti, now in his corner grocery; with Fred Borcher, now in his butcher shop; with Mr. and Mrs. Swenson, now wearing their red-and-white-striped jackets to match their ice cream parlor. There was also a dry cleaner's and a shoe store, where I could stick my bare feet on the metal plate of an X-ray machine, look through the rubber eyepiece and see my green, twiglike, vaporous bones. There was Sprouse Reitz, where I was apprehended by the manager, Herman Lynch, when I tried eating an Abba-Zaba behind the mossy, bubbling aquarium and the pyramid of slug bait. There was a clothing store where, without asking, I could make a beeline straight past boys' underwear, raise the lid of the white freezer and dig out a Neapolitan ice cream cup with a flat wooden spoon taped across it. Near the railroad station was a small, popular restaurant, Vic and Roger's, where we went almost every Friday night so my dad could order what he proclaimed were the best deep-fried prawns in California.

"As usual we're the only non-Catholics in the place," my mother would dryly comment from behind her seafood menu. One time we saw Miss Gita there with a man. Our waiter, when my mother asked, said he thought the man was her brother. "Poor soul." My mother trawled a fried shrimp through red cocktail sauce, "Don't you wonder how he got that way?"

"Fire," my father spoke through a mouthful, "or birth defect." He wiped his mouth with one of Vic and Roger's beige monogrammed napkins. "Could be both. Jaz, quit staring." For some inexplicable reason, my father had recently taken to calling me that. Jaz.

The only shop I hadn't been in (my mother always breezed disdainfully by) was a gift shop two doors down from Fred Borcher's, run, my mother said, by a Chinese couple who no doubt lived there, like those kind of people do. The shop didn't have a name, so I couldn't be sure it wasn't their living room window I was slowing down to stare into, a window displaying a dusty hodgepodge of European figurines—shepherdesses and lamplighters, embroidered red Chinese slippers, black lac-quered chopsticks, imported Irish tea towels and a row of white ceramic Buddhas, like pale, unmollified frogs. A scrim of amber-colored gel paper gave the display a dull, hot empty-aquarium look. Flies, upturned and skeletal, dotted the win-dow's edge. I stood counting them while Donna Rae, hands cupped to her eyes, surveyed the display case.

"No one goes in there," I offered lamely, but she was already pushing open the door. The shop's velvety dark interior smelled sweet with what Donna Rae later told me was Oriental incense. Now she was whispering that her mother always loved doing business with the Chinese in Livermore. As my eyes grew ac-customed to the darkness, I saw a lady standing behind a long glass counter, her mouth smudged with the same fuschia color as the rows of curlers in her hair.

Donna Rae spoke slowly, artificially. "We should like to see an item in your display case."

Not smiling, the woman stepped out from behind the counter and with a strange stick, like a pool cue with a metal hook, fished up, by its red cording, the clear plastic box Donna Rae had pointed to. She wore blue terry-cloth slippers, making me think my mother was right. These people lived here, and we were standing, two strangers, in their living room.

Donna Rae took the box, showing me what looked like a bunch of red-foil-wrapped bouillon cubes.

"Chocolate-covered bees," she whispered.

"Bees?" I leaned in to read the gold label.

"From Switzerland," the Chinese woman added.

"How much?" Donna Rae asked, sounding more herself.

"Seven dollars."

"Sorry, we have five."

The woman shook her head. Then, because he coughed, I noticed a man in the doorway leading into a back part of the store. They lived there, all right. For some reason, I remembered the joke Tiger Lindemann and Devlin Kuby had taken turns telling me, about a Chinaman, a barrel, and two straws.

"Look." Donna Rae ran one finger across the top of the box, lifting it to show the dust. The man's voice boomed cheerfully. "Five is OK."

Donna Rae turned to me, her hand out.

The silver dollars sagged, an anchor of resistance, in my shorts pocket. "Where's yours?"

"I haven't got it yet. Come on, Nors. I'll pay you back."

So there I was setting my large and valuable coins on the

glass countertop, everybody but me cheerful, smiling, pleased about the whole thing.

I started walking home, crossing to the opposite side of the street (that's how mad I was) before I remembered: dog food. Not looking at her, I recrossed and headed back to Fred Borcher's, took a number and waited, as always, by the organ meats, staring at the stainless-steel troughs of kidneys, brains, hearts, livers, the sallow waves of tripe. I had never eaten any of these things and wondered if I could. Fred, a tall man whose face reminded me of a tiny wooden mallet, winked as he handed over the dog food rolled in white butcher paper.

I got all the way to Balboa and Cortez before I saw Donna Rae. She was sitting beneath a maple tree, her perfect white legs stuck out, the gift box on her lap.

"Want to try one?" Her boldness as much as anything stopped me. She was undeterred by consequence, maybe even dishonest; still, I reminded myself, these were a far cry from courage.

"We can't. They're a gift."

"See these layers? We'll just take two off the bottom."

We sat unpeeling the red foil. We set the squares of Swiss chocolate into our opened mouths. Chinese bees, bees' knees. I waited to feel a leg, fuzz, the eyes, a head, something. There was only the slightest, bland crunch.

————————

I THAWED OUT a clump of George's dog food on my windowsill, wrote on my list that I had swallowed most of it, and by midnight was vomiting so violently my mother was convinced I had the summer flu she'd heard about. She refused to let me out of bed, much less out of the house to go to Miss Gita's. By noon she'd relented enough to let me sunbathe in the driveway. I was on my back, a pair of green plastic goggles over my eyes, my nose zinced, wearing one of her old suits, a purple one-piece, the built-in bust sticking up in the space between my chest and my collarbone, when I felt something longish and warm-blooded, like George, brush against my thigh. Propping up on my elbows, I blinked off the goggles, then screamed. Charging like a four-legged bullet for the utility room my dad had just built onto our old garage, the rat vanished. Within minutes, my dad was stalking it with a snow shovel while my mother, two steps behind, threatened to alert the county health department to the filthy Murphy premises, where no doubt they would find a ship's nest of rats. I picked up my beach towel and went inside to eat potato chips and wish I had stayed calm and courageous. Then the doorbell rang, and there was Donna Rae, in a frilly pink party dress, holding a large, adult-looking book on the Royal Ballet.

We sat in the wide stripe of shade on my front steps. I twiddled with the purple straps of my sagging suit and explained about getting sick and not being allowed to meet her. I told her about the rat. Donna Rae didn't seem interested, so I said, "It's a miracle I wasn't bitten. I could have gotten rabies and died."

"Miss Gita liked the bees."

"She ate them?"

"She's saving them for a special occasion." One step below me, Donna Rae glanced up with an expression I later identified as guilt.

"I'm going back for lunch tomorrow."

Here I spoke from a stupid assumption. "I don't have to wear a dress, do I?"

"Nors. I'm trying to tell you. I'm the only one invited."

"The only one? You didn't say the bees were from both of us? You didn't say that I bought them?"

Donna Rae had a finger deep in her mouth, prodding a loose tooth.

"You didn't even mention me, did you?" I saw myself in Miss Gita's Academy, pudgy, ugly, dodging behind Donna Rae. I stared at the book on the step, at the ballerina on its cover, brilliantly plumaged to look like a bluebird. She wore a hat like a bathing cap, made of blue sequins, with three white feathers sticking up. Dumb.

"If you want, you could come over now and we can . . ."

"No, thank you. I can't." *I have to stalk a rat.* After I locked the front door, I thought I heard the light, half-ringing thwang of a snow shovel. Then my mother was bullying pots and pans around the kitchen, her territory contaminated, and George, in there with her, had worked himself into a series of gruff, self-congratulatory barks.

Sunday had come and nearly gone. The church recessional, "Onward, Christian Soldiers," had boomed like a kettledrum through my blood all day. In the afternoon, I'd helped my mother iron handkerchiefs and polish the silver tea service that had been my great-aunt Mabel's and would one day be mine. I had eaten Sunday's pork roast and scrubbed the pan afterward, thinking it was a strange upbringing where you were expected to behave at prescribed times like a high-class person, then clean up after that person with your secondary servant self. Much later, I came to see this as the signature dynamic of the middle class, perpetually equipped for poverty, in sly practice for wealth.

Now it was dark and I was in the yard, stretched out on the striped, mildewy cushions of our old lawn-swing, an unopened package of Oreos on my lap. I was examining, with my flashlight, photographs of the Holocaust. How to react to this? For a while, I looked just at the faces, sometimes looking for Anne. But they were all Anne, and, of course, none of them was. How to react? I knew I wanted to be heroic. And underneath that, I wanted to be admired for that heroism, to be assured that beauty like Donna Rae's, even grace, weren't as noble or necessary as courage. I was in a state of great confusion. I believe I wept. The pictures shocked me, but there was also some other, personal hurt at work—mixed swells of emotion that had to do with feeling invisible, uncounted, in my own life.

My mother came out of the house and stood on the patio. I trained my flashlight on her.

"Eleanor Ann." Her arms were crossed on her chest. "Your friend is here to see you—at an inappropriate time, I might add." My flashlight picked out Donna Rae's white hair. She looked as if she was hiding behind my mother. I flipped the orb of light back down to my book and heard my mother go inside.

"Nors?" The swing rocked as she sat down on the far end. I drew my feet up and hoped an earwig bit her.

"Will you forgive me?"

"Why?"

"Because I believe you're smarter than me and you'll know what to do."

I closed the book and poked the light around to find her. Her face was puffy from crying. She wore an ugly shirt with big orange fish on it. She almost looked ordinary; and more impor- tant, she realized I was smarter than her.

"It's OK." The words were out before I knew if I meant them or was just curious. "What is it?"

First I heard about Miss Gita's hair, how, out of its bun, it fell straight to the floor and was a marbled white-and-gray color. Then she talked about Miss Gita's brother offering to drive her home, offering to buy her an ice cream (which she'd refused), offering to show her something and then taking that thing out of his pants while telling her what he wanted her to do—a thing she could never repeat to someone as innocent as I was—until she unlatched the car door, jumped out and hid in a hedge of lilac bushes. For the longest time, she said, he just sat there, playing the car radio. Finally he had driven off.

"Tell your father."

"My father? He'll never believe me."

"Why not?"

"I can't."

"You have to, Donna Rae."

"What if Miss Gita finds out?"

Exactly. A small, smug-but-obdurate voice spoke up in me. I became aware, for the first time, of saying the right thing for less than the right reason.

"Look. If Miss Gita finds out, I doubt it will kill her, but you can probably keep this from happening to anyone else."

"Weird stuff always happens to me." I heard her soft voice in the summer darkness and—later, upon reflection—wondered if she hadn't sounded just the slightest bit pleased.

OVER THE NEXT TWO DAYS, my mother, in one of her moods, put me to work in the front flower bed, tugging weeds, my hands stuck and sweating inside a pair of yellow rubber gloves. When Kristine Leipzig and Sandra Dougherty floated up the hilly bump of our lawn and stared down at me, a purposeful stare, as if they'd thought of a lot to say but had just lost their nerve, I kept churning up pieces of what I would later be informed had been a rare Japanese iris root. Finally, Sandra spoke. I had missed three meetings of the Katy Keene Fan Club. They hadn't done much, Kristine added, besides collect twenty-five cents from our one other member, Mitch Nasslund, a too-clutchy, bimbly kid with chronic toe-fungus who sought out the comparative refuge of girls. "Next meeting's Friday," Sandra informed me. I'd about decided the Katy Keene Fan Club was the most pointless thing I'd ever belonged to. I didn't even know who Katy Keene was. Nobody did, except Sandra, who once waved a couple of comic books about her in our faces. Bored by how I kept chipping away at the same iris root, by how little I had to say, Sandra and Kristine wafted down the lawn to the pavement and left me alone.

After lunch, I was helping my mother reorganize her upstairs linen closet—unfolding and refolding sheets, stacking them by color—when, without having rehearsed it, I asked if I could quit ballet. She snapped together the corners of one of our just-for-company bedsheets and held them between her teeth. "Eleanor Ann. Pick up your end. As for ballet, you have three more lessons paid for, and if your father and I succeed in teaching you anything, it's that money means commitment."

At that moment, George, who had been grinding away on his veal knuckle, sent up a nasal howl, *ahwoo-woo*ing out of his silvered snout. My mother, carrying a folded stack of fingertip towels, followed him. Looking out the bathroom window, she said, "Hell's bells. An ambulance at the Murphys'. That family is tragedy in a nutshell."

Two hours later I accompanied her, my hands in oven mitts, trying not to drop her salmon casserole, potato chips crushed like giant's dandruff all over the top. The oldest Murphy girl, who told us her name was Bridget, opened the door, still in her Catholic summer-school uniform. She said her mother had lost the baby and been taken—Mr. Murphy with her—to the hospital. Then Bridget took the Pyrex casserole dish, said thank you. Before she shut the door on us, I heard kids shouting, somebody practicing the piano, news blaring on the TV.

After our dinner, my mother relayed me back with a green Jell-O ring clogged with bits of canned fruit cocktail. I heard her tell my father she felt guilty for having reported the Murphys to the county health department the day before. Maybe because it was just me, Bridget invited me in, though she simply took the Jell-O and disappeared into the kitchen, where I could hear her talking on the phone. I sat by myself on a plastic-covered brown couch, sweat gathering under my knees, until a little boy, whose hair stood in strange orange peaks, like whipped squash, pulled me through the shambles of a kitchen, where I saw my mother's casserole on the counter, untouched. In a dim corner of the screened back porch, the boy knelt beside a cardboard box, stuffed his fingers, all five of them, into his mouth and started stroking the pale yellow down on the duckling nearest us. There were two. The other was tucked into a corner—asleep, I thought. Suddenly, an older girl, about eight, clattered onto the porch in a pair of red high heels, nipped the sleeping duckling by its neck and swung it out of the box. "Duckyduckyducky," she sang. The boy popped his fingers out of his mouth and started screaming. I noticed spots of blood in the box, that the duck's open eyes had a dull, blue film, and one side of its head was mostly a bloodied lump.

"Kathleen Elizabeth Murphy, I know what you're doing." Bridget's voice roared out from the house. "Put that poor tormented creature back this minute or I'll see you don't live till your ninth birthday."

The girl swung the duck by its neck once more before dropping it into the box and clomping back inside. In a fog of nausea and cowardice, I managed to say I had to go straight home. I ran through the backyard, unhooked the gate into the alley, and disgusted with myself, escaped into the relative peace of my own yard.

The following afternoon, Wednesday, I accidentally ripped a hole in the knee of my ballet tights and tried sealing it with my mother's red nail polish. I was late getting to our corner, and when I didn't see her, figured Donna Rae had gone ahead. I arrived at Miss Gita's, panting hard, the thick red blob tugging at the hairs on my knee. A woman named Betty Trower was teaching the class; Miss Gita, she said, was unwell. Noting Donna Rae's absence, I skidded to my place at the *barre* as Hayley Schmadabeck turned and glared at me. Betty Trower was wearing a purple leotard, and all her hair seemed to be jammed up inside a fat, purple turban. She complimented us. She praised us as if she were blind. She even refrained from ridiculing me, as Miss Gita surely would have, as I wobbled like a damaged top, trying to pirouette across the room. On my turn back, as I strained to exceed myself, my left arch gave way, and I hit the floor like a rock. As Miss Trower knelt and fussed extravagantly over my foot—in the process admitting she was really a jazz and tap teacher—I was inspired to say that whenever this happened, Miss Gita let me leave class early and walk home by myself.

COMING UP THE WEED-CHOKED WALKWAY, I already saw him in the overstuffed blue chair with the torn, ruffled hem. Sprawled, half-concealed behind a lattice losing its battle with an orange trumpet vine, Ray Earps had a can of beer propped on one knee and a cigarette, unlit, dangling from his lips. His head was tilted back, his eyes were shut. The porch was so small I stood right beside him, an anxious girl in a faded leotard and linty, red-splotted tights.

"Mr. Earps?"

He opened one eye.

"Is Donna Rae here?"

Now both eyes were open.

I raised my little plastic suitcase. "She missed class."

He picked the cigarette from his mouth, cleared his throat, set down his beer can, leaned and spat into the bushes.

"You're who now?"

"Her friend. Eleanor Stoddard."

"Well, Eleanor Stoddard, my daughter is no longer here." He looked at my face. "No longer at this residence."

Ray Earps stood up. He had no shirt on. His skin was tanned to bronze, and he looked nothing, in his half-nakedness, like my father.

"I put her on the Greyhound to Livermore yesterday morning, back to her mother." He looked sharply at me. "She didn't tell you? She said she did." His sigh was pained, yet unsurprised. "Hell, I'm sorry. Donna Rae's pretty ticked off at the truth. Meaning she rarely bothers to tell it. Let me get you a soda."

I followed Ray Earps, followed his broad, sweating back into the darkened house. I didn't really need a soda so much as I needed to see she was really gone. The news that June Earps was alive hadn't quite reached me yet. Halfway to the kitchen he turned, saw me looking down the hall.

"You leave something? Go ahead, go on in there."

The room was empty, but it had always been mostly empty; it just felt different. The kitchen chair was gone, and the candles—so were all the ballet words I'd helped thumbtack to the walls, except for one still stuck to the back of the closet door, *relevé* (re-le-VAY). I was passing my hand back and forth under the pillow to see if June Earps's picture was still there when I heard footsteps and sat down.

Ray Earps sat beside me and handed me a can of grape soda. "That stuff's too sweet, I don't know how you kids stand it. Now here's the deal. Donna Rae'd come to live with me for the summer; then on Sunday I believe it was, she woke me up with another of her cockamamie stories—this one about her ballet teacher's brother . . . you know anything about that, she tell you about that, Eleanor?"

"No, sir," I lied so fast it startled me. "No, sir." I dug in deep. "She never did." My gaze traveled up to the red truck.

"Is that your son's?"

"My son? No, that old fire truck belonged to my younger brother, who died when he was four. For some reason Donna Rae's always been partial to keeping it in her room."

"Could she touch it?"

"What do you mean?"

"Could she touch the truck?"

"Sure she could. I just told her the special nature of it and to be careful when she did."

"She told me it was her brother's and she wasn't supposed to ever touch it and that he had died. She told me your wife was dead, too." By now I was doing two things, picking off the scab of polish on my knee and starting to cry. "She told me they'd died in a car wreck."

"She told you that?" He rested his hand on the part of my back that was bare. Neither of us said anything for a while.

"Donna Rae's mother and I got our divorce a year ago. She is remarried and lives there in Livermore. As for a brother, Donna Rae doesn't have any brothers or sisters. She got herself into some trouble, telling lies about her stepfather, so I told June she was welcome to stay here with me, though I made it clear my place wasn't anything like hers, no Doughboy pool, no red T-bird convertible, nothing like that. But like I said before, Donna Rae, especially since her mom and I split up, runs farther and farther from the truth. It's like she makes things up to be the way she wants. Maybe it comes from having a drama teacher as a mother. An actress. I told her—one day, it's going to catch up to you, you're going to find yourself or get somebody else in deep trouble. Now this business about a man in a car. She's cried wolf on me one too many times, that's the last thing I said to her, her currency's about used up in that department. So I figured the best thing was to put her on a bus back to Livermore. Get her out of Dodge. Then again, maybe it wasn't the right thing. Maybe the guy really did do what she said. I find it hard to believe. I find Donna Rae hard to believe. Hell, you tell me."

He walked across the floor and stood staring out the window. I had stopped crying and was frankly studying the way his blond hair tailed down the nape of his neck, the muscled, triangular slope of his back. It was male beauty I was looking at, sexual attraction, though I had no words or any real feeling for it then.

"It's nearly dark. You live close or do you need a ride?"

"I live close."

"Thing is . . ." Here he turned and looked right at me. "June, my wife—my ex-wife—is the most beautiful woman in the world to me. The only woman. And you know what's funny? One day, some joker, some other clown who I should already start feeling sorry for but I won't, is going to feel that same way about Donna Rae. About my own daughter. What I'm talking about here is time."

I nodded as if I understood. Then he was lifting the can of soda from my hands, his face so close, the smell of beer so strong, I flinched.

"I would lay down my life for that woman. I've already tried. And to do that for someone who doesn't give a rat's ass about you—it hurts. It plain hurts. I won't get over this, Eleanor Stoddard."

Only then, as he started to cry, did it occur to me how drunk he really was.

I followed him back outside. The house had been so dark and sad that even the porch at dusk seemed bright. Before he could land back in his chair, I put my hand out like I had seen my father do.

"Thank you very much, Mr. Earps."

He took my hand, startled. Whatever else I'd thought to say

scattered as I looked into his eyes. Ray Earps was courtly and wounded, poor and self-pitying, sensitive and too-handsome, the kind of man I would zero in on for years. But I didn't know that then. I only knew how my heart felt, losing its race, how ridiculous I looked in my leotard, how his hand felt with mine, how we were bound by one sweet, irresistible pain.

I started for home, half expecting to see my mother out driving around, looking for me. So when the car slowed behind me on the quiet street and I didn't hear her voice, I turned to see instead Miss Gita's shark-finned old Cadillac, and hunched over the wheel, staring straight at me, her brother.

I don't remember. I must have had some instinct to run or to scream. Instead, and to this day I don't know why, I did the strangest thing, deliberately, as if obeying the shape of dreams. Backing away until I stood on someone's green lawn, not taking my eyes off the accused, I raised both arms—fingertips touching, *port de bras*; pointing my left foot, *tendu*; striking it twice against the grass, *frappé*; and began to turn. My figure whirled, turning, darkness both supporting and concealing it, until the Cadillac was a blur, until it was gone, until with a sharp, exhilarating cramp in my ribs I ran for home. My mother, who had been taking a nap, had not even missed me.

ON FRIDAY I SHOWED UP in Sandra Dougherty's backyard, quieter than usual, drank lemonade out of a Dixie cup, handed over twenty-five cents for the fan club. I took my turn touching

Kristine Leipzig's newest patch of psoriasis on her elbow; I laughed at Mitch Nasslund's stupid Chinaman jokes, the two he knew. I tried to forget what I had been thinking about for days—that something lay dormant inside each of us, that only the right constellation of weaknesses could bring whatever it was into the light. And that keeping those weaknesses separated from one another was probably all anyone ever meant by being good.

I returned the Holocaust books, but not before tearing up my childish list and stuffing the bits inside one of them. I began walking past Ray Earps's house every single evening. I had fantasies of being his perfect daughter, or wife, depending. Miss Gita had recovered from the summer flu, and I refused to go to my last two classes. I was punished but did not care. I sat in my room and thought about the ballet suitcase I had left at Ray Earps's house that day, how the time would come for me to go over there and get it back and that I would know when that time came. I stopped reading and did not read again until seventh grade, and then only what I was assigned. My father complained I watched too much TV, though my mother was pleased I was losing weight, walking for exercise, paying more attention to my femininity. The truth is, things had happened, and it helped to blame other people.

I was no longer comfortable with the way Fred Borcher looked at my mother or the way she laughed at his jokes. One day, when I asked, she explained she had been a Catholic until she eloped with my father, after which she was excommunicated. According to her former priest, I, as the fruit of their marriage, was banned for eternity from paradise. I noticed how often my father worked late and, even when he was home, seemed away. I continued to have fantasies about Ray Earps, wrote love poems and letters and stuffed them into a suitcase under my bed. Before long I would be reading again, books I was embarrassed to check out or to bring home. So I stayed at the library, what I chose to read concealed inside more acceptable books. I was catching up to Donna Rae; I would surpass her, for beauty was not to be my protector, nor did I aspire, as I once had through false tests, to courage.

The more I would learn to shape myself into the kind of woman I imagined Ray Earps might grieve over and want to die for (though I was never to see him again—he would take his own life the following Christmas), the more he would become the shadow behind all the boys and men I would open my arms to, *port de bras,* on my back where I thought I belonged and wanted to be, for all those years, passionate and grasping and full of delusion, to come.

Salve Regina

Every angel is terrifying.

RAINER MARIA RILKE

Eleanor Stoddard tightened the scarlet strip with its notchings of white numbers around her naked hips. After two weeks of traversing the bedroom floor on her rear end—one hip thrusting out then the other, "walking" back and forth, back and forth—tonight's measurement mocked all her efforts. Stuffing the measuring tape into her ballerina jewelry box, Eleanor doused a cotton square with Bonnie Bell 1006, and drove it up and down her face as if she were cleaning a rug. She performed the eye-widening exercises Lacey had shown her, convinced she was doing them backwards. Lacey liked to describe her own eyes as hopeless, small and too gray, like wet, dead guppies. Dropping on a rosebud-sprigged nightie, Eleanor skewered empty beer cans on her head, two on top, one on each side, three down the back, so her hair, by tomorrow morning, might almost resemble Lacey's.

Eleanor snapped off all the lights except the yellow bean-pot lamp on her nightstand. She's hated this room ever since her mother redecorated it in marigold yellows and orange, with the baffling and pointless theme of Spain. Directly over Eleanor's bed hung a framed travel poster showing a matador in pink balletic shoes, poised to gore a bull, ESPAÑA written in red letters down one side. Her only option was to ignore her surroundings, as if she were stranded in some foreign, second-rate motel. Now, removing her glasses and dropping to her knees, Eleanor began a fervent series of prayers to the Blessed Virgin Mary as set forth by Reverend Mother Stewart in one of her pocket-sized booklets distributed by Holy Rood Press in Long Island. If Eleanor's dispute with her flesh had ended in yet another rout, then her will to acquire saintliness seemed, if only by mulish reaction, to be accelerating.

MO AND MITZI STODDARD, Eleanor's parents, went on being pleased with last year's decision to send their only child, in her sophomore year, to a private school. Without appearing prejudiced, they had neatly sidestepped the issue of public school integration. Removing their daughter from a politically volatile climate ensured Eleanor a superior education at the hands of nuns said to be the female equivalent of Jesuits. The Convent of the Sacred Heart was academically rigorous, the architecture impressive, the grounds parklike and secluded. And though she had never been to Europe, Mitzi exclaimed that the Convent looked like something you would surely drive past in France, certainly in Paris, where the mother school, Sacre Coeur, was said to still exist. This local convent was attended mainly by the daughters of wealthy capitalists, Catholics naturally, many of whom were boarders. Eleanor, neither a Catholic nor a boarder, rode her Sears bicycle to and from school each day.

Although there had been the possibility of a second private school in San Francisco, the Stoddards deemed it less costly, wiser, to keep Eleanor home. Mo particularly wanted to supervise his daughter's orthodontia. As a dentist, the alignment of her teeth was of professional and even competitive concern to him. Mitzi felt this a little silly, overinvolved, but didn't think it politic to complain. After all, hadn't she met Morris when he had appeared with a group of dental students at the tooth factory in Scranton? Few people, the tour guide had said, stopping to ogle Mitzi, could appreciate the skill involved, sorting and matching teeth. As if on cue, Mitzi had glanced up from her task of pairing three hundred adult male incisors and paralyzed Mo, or so he would forever claim, by smiling directly, blazingly, at him. People didn't realize, the guide continued, how many thousands of teeth, made here in Scranton, were shipped overseas—even as the demand for false teeth dropped in the United States, other parts of the world, England especially, where people lost as many teeth as ever. In the midst of this, Mo and Mitzi exchanged phone numbers. Eventually they married and moved to California, where Mitzi embarked upon the long and occasionally gratifying process of reinventing herself. The Stoddards were Goldwater Republicans, members of the Menlo Country Club, and Mitzi herself kept up with several vaguely prestigious volunteer activities as well as her monthly bridge group, referred to affectionately by its eight members as "Sherry and Therapy."

Mitzi Stoddard had done well; at the moment, fifteen-year-old Eleanor was her single vexation. The child was stiff-limbed, morose, socially regressive. Stepping into Eleanor's room yesterday afternoon to put up the Costa Brava travel poster she'd had reframed in yellow, Mitzi literally stumbled over an untidy heap of religious paraphernalia sticking out from under the orange chenille bedspread. A gloomy-looking black-and-silver rosary, half a dozen dog-eared prayer booklets written in zealous purple prose, three holy cards—one with the image of a crown of thorns wrapped around a heart spurting blood—and, of all dreary things, a cheap black face veil. She didn't dare tell Morris.

In the best of times, Mo referred to himself as an agnostic; in the worst, a hard-boiled cynic. His moods hinged entirely upon the state of his practice. What no one had warned her about was that dentists, after psychiatrists, had the highest rate of suicide. This terrified Mitzi, so she worked to keep her husband at a constant temperature, like a coddled egg. She had overcome his loudest objection to sending Eleanor to a convent, saying she would see to it that Eleanor did not convert, turn into a nun or a missionary in Calcutta; nothing religiously untoward would occur. Now this. Face veils. Rosaries. Thorns poking into hearts.

On a lesser note, Mitzi held out optimism that in a school of girls all wearing the same dull, triangular blue skirts and god-awful cropped boleros (uniforms imported from Cairo, Egypt, for pity's sake), Eleanor's homeliness would hardly distinguish itself. Behind convent walls, she might outgrow her ugly-ducklingness.

RIDING HER BICYCLE to school that first morning after Christmas vacation, Eleanor wore her new black knit cap and mittens. The brilliant winter air left her cheeks flushed and her eyes watering as she cycled past the gold-lettered sign, Sacre Coeur, past the spiked ironwork gates of the convent, as if she were departing one way of life, even one century, for another. The serpentine road she cycled along, bordered by semicircular beds of sky-blue agapanthus and half-wild rose hedges splashed with scarlet, was irregularly shaded by thick stands of oak and feathery palms with regal, supple-seeming gray trunks. Eleanor rode up to the three-story building made of rose-colored granite with its great columned porte cochere, its crenellated towers and cupolas, feeling, spiritually at least, by way of sanctuary and relief, home. The Sacred Heart religious presided over their domain with the same century-old discipline established by the mother school in Paris. Theirs was a serene, fastidious government, the school and its vast estate sealed, as if under a bell jar, in an atmosphere rich and seductive, faintly erotic, where school rituals were called by their French names: *prime, gouter, congé.* By contrast, the Stoddard's house was a show of modern, one-dimensional conformity. Neighbors commented on how well-kept it was, but to Eleanor her home seemed an arid, card-house imbued with anxiety; indeed, she could scarcely distinguish its square rooms from her father's bland dental suites.

Leaving her bicycle in the small rack by the kitchen, Eleanor ascended a set of side stairs and went into the building. Passing the library, she went up yet another set of wide, red-carpeted stairs to the second floor, where she slipped into an alcove, knelt on a plain, wooden prie-dieux and gazed up at the seated, life-size figure of the Virgin. On an altar banked by green glass vases of thickly fleshed white lilies, Mary's indigo mantle fell in solemn, anchored folds over her pale rose gown. The twelve stars of the Apocalypse encircled her humbly inclined head, and her canted gaze—Eleanor always felt it personally—was tender, brimming, enigmatic. The Virgin saw nothing, saw without judgment into the heart of everything.

Remember, O Most Gracious Virgin Mary, that never was it known, that anyone who fled to thy protection, implored thy help or sought thy intercession was left unaided. Inspired by this confidence I fly to thee, O Virgin

of virgins, my mother; to thee I come, before thee I stand,
sinful and sorrowful. O Mother of the word incarnate, de-
spise not my petitions, but in thy mercy hear and answer
me. Amen.

Eleanor left the alcove and stealthily went downstairs to the chapel. One of her most frequent prayers was to please not be seen in either place. The nuns would surely press for conversion, and the other girls, even Lacey, most of all Lacey, jaded from years of Catholic schooling, might tease her, or worse. The way the two queer girls were shunned was instruction enough. Rose and Deirdre. Eleanor had never spoken to them. Marooned on an ugly spar of talk, they clung tightly to the wreckage of one another, incurring further derision. No one actually knew if they were queer or not—rumor itself condemned them. On occasion, Eleanor prayed for their souls, but like everyone else, she was repulsed by their cowed, doughy faces, their moist, nail-bitten hands, their downcast expressions of shame. Eleanor had a secret terror of being like them. Not that she was queer, surely not—half the girls in the school had a crush on Mother Fitzgerald, she wasn't alone in that. It was this other, increasing devotion to Mary, to the Virgin (whose image Eleanor generally mixed up with Mother Fitzgerald's), that caused her to feel generally outcast and mildly disgraced. In the middle of her third academic year, Eleanor could not help being what she was, a diligent girl. Respected but plain. Never left out, never first to be included. Nun's pet. A model girl, intelligent, obedient, dull as dust.

Shortsighted even with her glasses, Eleanor, as she walked into the darkened chapel, made out a large, vague object—a table or so she thought—set before the altar. She walked straight up to it. The nun's freckled hands were modestly crossed, a plain black rosary wrapped around them, her black habit and white wimple stiff and pleated, a pair of gold pince-nez placed (as if she would need them!) over her closed eyes. She looked like a small human made of paper or a large doll made of powdered, papery flesh. With her heart flaring, Eleanor raced from the chapel, bolted up two flights of stairs to the study hall, and entered, breathless, from the back door just as Mother Fitzgerald, Mistress of Studies for the third and fourth academics, swept in from the front, her black skirts and long, sheer veil pulsing with sensual vitality behind her.

The third-floor study hall was a high-ceilinged room, its cream-colored walls trimmed with varnished oak wainscoting. A row of tall, deeply recessed windows along the room's north side overlooked Palm Court, a circular patio area shaded by palm trees, where, during the more clement months of April and May, the girls ate their lunch, and in June, each year's graduating class held a small but elegant commencement ceremony.

Inside the pocket of her habit—designed after a nineteenth-century French mourning costume—Mother Fitzgerald carried a palm-sized mahogany clapper, an instrument brought out and clicked in the manner of castanets, not with any rhythm of course, but to command silence, attention, obedience. She now used her clapper, as briskly and confidently as she did everything. As she mounted the platform and stood to one side of her wooden lectern, flanked by the American flag and large color photographs of John F. Kennedy Jr. and Pope John XXIII, Mother Fitzgerald surveyed the sixty or so blue-uniformed girls seated before her. She was aware that some of them were infatuated with her, though none more so, or more obviously, than Eleanor Stoddard. She had been receiving small, delicately folded notes from Eleanor for weeks now, usually discussing points of theology. Mother Fitzgerald interpreted these as camouflaged love notes. Accustomed to receiving such notes from girls, along with sly, hot glances and small gifts, tokens of affection, she prayed regularly to be forgiven the deep sense of pleasure these aroused in her. She reminded herself that her main task was to take a misguided love and direct it to its true source, God. Still, and she felt some thrilling shame over this, she had saved each letter, each note, sweet evidence of her students' affection for her, in a small pine box with a key.

The girls, she announced, were to proceed down to chapel, where they were to attend a funeral mass for Mother Logan, who had been living these past nine years in the nuns' retirement home. The convent's property was quite immense; beyond the main building, the girls were restricted to the tennis courts, hockey field, swimming pool and, on special occasions, the school's religious gardens, a damp disorienting maze of grottoes where stained marble statues of St. Agnes, St. Joseph, Mater, Our Lady of Lourdes, all with voluptuous yet stern expressions, were enshrined then forgotten. None of the girls had ever been inside the retirement home, none of them knew Mother Logan. They were, said Mother Fitzgerald, her cheeks turning their irresistible rose color, to retrieve their missals and veils from their desks and form ranks. The ordinary school day, she added with a small, reassuring smile, would resume after Mass.

THEY FILED PAST the closed coffin and, with black veils covering their young faces, knelt to receive communion. Eleanor sat alone, listening to the elderly nuns in the front two pews sing *"Salve Regina"* in rehearsed, silvery unison. Mantled in black, diminutive and round-shouldered, most wore the same gold pince-nez as Mother Logan and they seemed to have the same parsnip pallor. Except that they were upright, open-eyed, and harmonizing, Eleanor thought they were no different from their now-dead companion. She could never imagine Mother Fitzgerald becoming this, turning into this, could not imagine everything distinctive and vitally exquisite about her stripped away. Perhaps that was the point. Perhaps it was a fact of becoming old. One's personality fell away.

———

CARRYING A BATCH of essays on martyrdom to Reverend Mother's office as a favor for Mother Fitzgerald, Eleanor was surprised to see the crèche still in place weeks after Christmas. At the beginning of Advent, each girl's name was typed and glued, a paper girth, around the midsection of a small woolen lamb. The lambs, sixty or so, stood in a solid, snowy bank on the long bottom step of a series of shallow, green-felted stairs leading up to the manger. By Christmas Eve, they were all to have reached the top step, to assemble meekly before the holy family. But throughout the season, infractions of rules, the most minor lapses in conduct, were taken note of by the nuns until the flock was broken into punished, straggling ranks. A wild, re-fractory few lagged four or more steps behind. Eleanor's lamb, as it had the year before, ascended without incident or inter-ruption to Jesus. Lacey Jenks's was detained five steps down, gazing sideways toward the lavatory, where she had twice been caught smoking. Far from being chastened, Lacey had laughed. She had been obedient for too many years, and where in the world, she asked Eleanor, had it gotten her?

Eleanor met Lacey Jenks at the fall tea her first year at Sacred Heart. Lacey had been appointed as Eleanor's "Angel," to watch over and guide her. Despite Eleanor's resolution never to laugh at the expense of others, she took immediate, guilty pleasure in her new friend's humor, a sly, sometimes sniping wit fed by unerring perception. It was Lacey who first pointed out that the backs of Madame Sesiche's legs were unshaven—you could see them when she turned to conjugate active and passive verbs on the blackboard—and that the music appreciation teacher, Miss Trammel, was going bald on top of her head, a plight she failed to disguise with tortoiseshell barrettes and artful shiftings of her part. And it was Lacey who told her about Mother Fitzgerald, who, it was rumored, the night before her wedding to the son of a Greek prince, took refuge in the convent, where she has been ever since.

Though it was never spoken of, another factor bound these two. Both Eleanor and Lacey rode bicycles to school, both were reminded in constant, subtle ways by their parents that private school was a privilege, that sacrifices were being made. The boarders, on the other hand, accustomed to an unvarying climate of wealth, were oblivious, even careless of its intimidating effect on girls like Eleanor and Lacey. No one spoke of money, yet friendships fell plainly along economic lines. The wealthier girls kept to themselves, while girls like Lacey and Eleanor found themselves unexpectedly and sometimes fiercely compatible.

From the very beginning, Mitzi had been unhappy with Eleanor's Angel. Lacey Jenks was a day student, her mother a city librarian, her father a retired army colonel. They lived in an older, slightly run-down section of Menlo Park. Why couldn't Eleanor have gotten one of the other girls, one of the Dial soap heiresses, for instance? While she tolerated the friendship between her daughter and this Lacey, she did little to encourage it. Several of the other girls Eleanor invited home at different times seemed pleasant enough, but these, too, Mitzi ascertained from a few calculated inquiries, were less than sterling liaisons. The task fell to Mitzi to chip out an acceptable social niche for her daughter. Currently, through her connections at the Menlo Country Club, she was lobbying for Eleanor's invitation to the upcoming cotillion. Were she to attend, her name might well appear in the society column of the *San Francisco Chronicle,* linked with those of local debutantes. She was horrified to see, however, that Eleanor's complexion was worsening. The crescent-shaped rash of pimples around her chin was migrating up toward her temples. Mo would have to agree to getting her into weekly acne treatments again. Though it gave Eleanor's skin something of the suggestion of a bad sunburn, the ultraviolet light worked wonders. Besides, Mitzi enjoyed flirting with the dermatologist, Dr. Ferraye. Flirting stabilized a marriage, and Mitzi had long been aware when she "dolled up"—Mo's phrase—to do her errands, men eagerly attended her and things got done. She wished Eleanor could understand the efficiency, the pragmatism of beauty.

Dear Boobs,

Merci for your letter. I'm in a poopy mood but you're not ugly. You'd blush if you knew how cute you are. For lunch I had two pieces of white bread, one lamb and

*gravy, one peanut butter and jelly. Thing of jello, five
round teeny crackers, 500 cal. or more, ergo: no dinner.
Ughy Ughy. Helen just asked me if I was writing an en-
cyclopedia. What does life mean—what is love—I want
to find out this weekend—Does Mother F. really hate
me?—Miss Trammel forgot to put on D.O.—I am a
boob—I think I shall take down my girdle and go to pot.
I hate you cause you're everything I wish I could and
should be—I have a hate complex. Am I a boob? Do I
look like a boob? Helen is upset cause I won't let her
read this and she thinks I am writing nasties about her.
Je ne sais quoi.*

    I love you with all my toe. Respectful au revoirs,
    One Little Boob

Such notes to Eleanor had begun to change. Since the
onset of her guitar lessons, Lacey's notes were dominated by
someone named Arthur Webb. Even her handwriting grew
crimped and stupidly curlicued. For Christmas, her parents had
succumbed and given Lacey a Sears guitar along with six
months of paid lessons. Classical lessons, not what she'd
wanted, but as she told Eleanor, how else would she ever have
met Arthur? Her first lesson was at Kepler's, a small, popular
music store in downtown Menlo Park. Arthur, she wrote
Eleanor, had taken her into a tiny, white soundproof cubicle and
sitting inches away, demanded she open her legs wide, no much

wider, like so, the guitar had to lie properly across her lap. He made her sing "On Top of Old Smokey" without any accompaniment, in order to get, he said, some idea of her pitch. The whole time she was singing he'd stared at her, his eyes narrowed. Arthur was a graduate student at San Francisco State College, and Lacey thought he was twenty-three or -four, though she'd never asked. She'd brought a news clipping to show Eleanor, a minuscule announcement of a recital, with his picture. But Eleanor couldn't tell much; his face was blurred. The impression she got was of two mournful eyes and a great mop of dark shaggy hair. Twice Lacey asked Eleanor to come to the music shop, but Eleanor, reticent, embarrassed, said no. Much later, she would wish she had gone, had seen them together, but some part of her dug in, was mad. She missed the old notes, the sly, catty ones, the ones that made her laugh so hard she could only hope to be forgiven.

A second tiresome consequence of Lacey's "romance" was her constant absorption in her appearance. From one day to the next her hair changed, her diet altered, her mood swung. By contrast, Eleanor's acne worsened; she'd stopped bottom "walking"; and her hair, minus Mo's empty beer cans, hipped out on the sides and dwindled like a dying plant on top. Though one day, after flipping through an issue of *Seventeen* (for Christmas—a stocking stuffer—Mitzi had given her a year's subscription), she rubbed her lips with talcum powder, then smeared Vaseline over them, an inexpensive trick, the article promised, to get that ethereal English look. Over dinner, Mo har-harred that his daughter looked next in line for Rasputin's Funeral Home. Mitzi tried shushing him, but Eleanor fled to her room and whammed the door. Alone with Mitzi's wrath, Mo waggled his eyebrows and made an O with his mouth, a ridiculous expression intended to absolve him.

So while Lacey practiced guitar scales, her fingertips turning white with callus and slightly bloodied—for Arthur, she'd sigh—Mitzi got Eleanor a volunteer job at Stanford Hospital. Now she wore a second uniform, a bibbed, red-and-white seersucker jumper with white sneakers. She assisted new mothers, helped them into wheelchairs, handed over their newborn infants, rolled them into an elevator, then out to the curb where husbands waited beside the family car like soldiers, like doormen or butlers, like nervous new fathers. Eleanor held each infant as the mother was helped by her husband into the car, then leaned down to hand over the small bundle. What made these people trust her with an infant? What if she dropped it, what if it rolled under the car? She told Lacey the husbands always insisted on a picture of her holding the baby, standing beside the new mother in her wheelchair. Why would they want a picture like that? Eleanor imagined herself appearing in photo albums of strangers all over the state of California. As a candy striper, she liked the sanitized cheerfulness of the hospital; she liked helping people who invariably expressed curious gratitude for what she found intolerably awkward, her own youth. Eventually,

Eleanor would receive a red-and-white-enameled pin for working one hundred hours; this would be noted in a small column of the hospital newsletter. "Goody Two-shoes," Lacey teased. "Nora Brownnoser. Wait until Reverend Mother plops one of her ribbons on you." Lacey was referring to honor ribbons awarded at the school ceremony known as Prime: satin sashes crossing the chest and shoulders, fastened at the hip with a small, bronze medal. Eleanor did want a pale blue sash across her chest, placed there by Reverend Mother McGwynn, in front of the whole school, as a sign of her exemplary behavior.

How, the Stoddards agreed, could you fault a child for taking life seriously? Mo was mainly relieved she had not picked up what he called the God bug. Mitzi tried to be proud of her daughter—she understood she should be. Still, she didn't care for studiousness, for this sort of earnestness in a young girl. Ambition wasn't feminine; it frightened people. And privately, Mitzi equated religion with moral insurance for the old or dying. Regularly, she checked Eleanor's room. The gloomy articles were still there. Some nights, unable to sleep, she pictured Eleanor announcing a vocation. She and Mo would have to drive out to some godforsaken cloister somewhere to visit their former daughter, now Mother Stoddard, sitting behind bars, prim, humorless, bespectacled. No wedding. No grandchildren. Mitzi would instead bring boxes of unscented soap, rough washcloths, sets of plain homespun underwear. It was her worst nightmare. She had read enough about teenagers to understand you couldn't confront them directly. You couldn't even agree with them. The best strategy was to feign indifference to whatever wrong direction they were headed in, then plop in little facts, like Alka-Selzers, round innocuous comments. Let those sink in, take slow, antidotal effect: On average, nuns die a full fifteen years before normal women . . . Nuns cannot take vacations . . . Have you ever seen a nun on a roller coaster or riding a horse . . . ? Nuns can't dance or marry or swim in the sea . . . Imagine, up at three every morning, grinding away at the same silly prayers, rain or shine, year in, year out. Casually, Mitzi tapped out such little notions of monotony, usually when they were driving somewhere. And though Eleanor never said a word, never responded, Mitzi never gave up hope.

Eleanor was responding. She saw what her mother was up to—persecution. Each night, on her knees beneath the picture of the pink-slippered matador, Eleanor begged for a vision. Sometimes she felt translucent, as though light were pouring through her, as though the air around her were heavy as syrup and she herself were light, porous, all her weight vanishing into her soul and flying upward. She counted these among the happiest sensations she had known.

With the latest note crumpled in her hand (*Noser: Music Room, 12:30, News!*), she found Lacey sitting on the piano bench, her face ignited by the as yet undisclosed "news." Stealthily, Eleanor shut the door behind her. No doubt this had to do with what's-his-face, Arthur Webb.

"Come over to me, Noser. Close your eyes. Are they closed? OK."

Eleanor stood blind in the center of the small practice room, her hands loosely clasped behind her back. First she felt Lacey's hands on her shoulders, smelled her gingery breath, then came the kiss—brief, warm, lovely.

The piano bench dragged on the floor a little. Lacey plinked a bit of "Heart and Soul," softly, on the piano.

"Eleanor. Open your eyes. Do they look different? My lips? God, I needed to call you, but I didn't want the Colonel eavesdropping, which he would, the big boob. And I didn't dare write anything in case someone else read it. Oh my God. Yesterday, after my lesson, Arthur kissed me. He's been wanting to since the first time he saw me. That's what he said."

Eleanor thought Lacey's lips looked unchanged, maybe drier. She'd assumed Arthur didn't know what Lacey felt about him, or, if he did know, wouldn't care. After all, he was twenty-three or -four and went to college. She and Lacey weren't even sixteen. Now Lacey was pursing her lips and rolling her eyes in the most asinine way.

"You shouldn't do that."

"Why, Nors? He loves me. He's practically said so."

"The man is older than you. Not to mention he's your teacher."

"So? I'm sixteen in two months. We've already decided to wait."

"Wait for what?"

"Honest to God, Stoddard. Don't be dense. To have sex. Arthur is mature, and he's got this friend who's got a place at the beach we . . ."

"Lacey will you stop? I can't hear this anymore."

"Why? I've been talking to you for months."

Eleanor was sure their absence from Study Hall had been noticed, that they were about to be caught, that because of Lacey she would lose her chance for a ribbon.

"I'm sorry if I'm boring you. There's just no one else I can trust with this. I trust you with my life, Nors. I promise to talk about Arthur less. Not one word. I won't use any word that starts with A. I'll . . ."

"Lacey. We've got to get back to Study Hall."

"OK, OK. We're gone. We're there. What about this? If I promise not to say another word about A (she silently mouthed his name), can I still give you a signal that says we've done it? Had sex?"

Eleanor found herself agreeing just to get out of the music room. And for the next three weeks, Eleanor did get a respite from his name, did get some part of their old, Arthur-less relationship back, at least until the signal came, a silly, double thumbs-up, after which nothing was the same.

ON THE SAME NIGHT Lacey Jenks was to lose her virginity in, of all places, Kepler's music shop (there was no friend's beach house, nothing like that, only a ratty old maroon sofa in the back, where Arthur had already seduced two other girls—he was beginning to think he had a knack for this), on that same evening, Mitzi Stoddard was putting the finishing touches on Eleanor. Considering the obstacles she'd climbed over, one damned thing after another, she had a right to feel pleased. The biggest obstacle had turned out to be Mo, who was in one of his funks. His practice was down—he had lost three clients in one month—though Mitzi reminded him two of the three had died, which could hardly be taken personally, and the third was Sam Widdle, so a high, holy good riddance. But Mo took anything to do with his dentistry to heart, and what Mitzi didn't know was he had also made investments without consulting her and was steadily losing money on them. (In fact, if Mitzi lifted the lid on what a kettle of fish he was in, she would throw a fit—exactly why he hadn't told her. They would have to shag his broken keester down some long, lonesome road, creditors braying all the way, before he'd unload his troubles to her. All he could bring himself to suggest was that Mitzi keep the expenses down to a dull roar.) And Mitzi, ever nervous about his statistical weakness for suicide, accepted a friend's loan of her daughter Helen Marie's cotillion dress from last year. Both girls, it turned out, wore the same size, and the dress, while nondescript, was at least a Lanz original. So she had only to pay for Eleanor's hair and a pair of white brocade pumps she found at Payless and had dyed emerald green.

So now her daughter—fifteen!—stood before her, wearing a midcalf, white chiffon dirndl skirt with a sleeveless gold lamé top, in emerald heels with a dyed-to-match purse, a wide, emerald velveteen bow perched slightly past the crown of her head, her hair professionally done—to match Mitzi's—in a lacquered, bouffant flip.

"Morris!" This came gaily from Eleanor's bedroom. "Picture time!"

Helmet head. Freakdoody. With strangely reticent bitterness, Eleanor regarded her reflection. Her own mother could not see how tacitly ugly she had become, how ready she was to die.

Mo shambled in with the camera, picked his unlit cigar out of his mouth, told his daughter that orthodontia aside, she was an eyeful. Indeed she did look almost dazzling, reminding him of Mitzi when he'd first seen her—"You have got to be the Tooth Fairy," he'd teased, partly to hide how defenseless he'd suddenly felt. Now he noticed even Eleanor's acne had been cleverly camouflaged.

"Gorgeous, Jaz. Let me get some pictures, record this moment for future generations, huh?" A comment which, as soon as he made it, depressed him. A future generation implied his own absence. In the living room, he took the obligatory pictures in front of the fireplace and the picture window. He snapped several of Mitzi and Eleanor together, pictures Mitzi would crunch into a ball and plunge into the trash when she saw how, next to her daughter, she looked at least a decade older than she felt.

"Ready for the ball, Cindyfella?" Mo joked, and with that chauffeured Eleanor to her first and last cotillion, a cramp in her left toe, her mouth aching from having had her braces tightened that morning.

At the expansively lit entrance to the Menlo Country Club, Eleanor got out of her father's new red Mustang, stood there a moment, leaned down and asked, "Can I come home now?"

Poor kid, Mo thought. I should take her out for a hamburger and a movie, let her mother think she went to this monkey-ass thing. But Mitzi was waiting. She had a surprise, she'd winked almost lewdly from the garage as he backed the Mustang out, and he knew, or hoped he knew, what that meant. The sight of his daughter maturing into a woman made him remember his own and Mitzi's youth—what was it called, splendor in the grass?—and he found himself excited about the how and when and where of her surprise. Would she be hiding stark naked in the laundry room, or wearing some flimsy negligee, waving a bottle of champagne and two glasses—things she had done before—these memories, and possibilities distracted him and he started to answer his daughter by saying "Oh, ten, eleven, twelve," when he saw Eleanor's pleading, myopic expression. He really ought to find a way to finance contact lenses for her.

"Nine-thirty should make your mother happy. You just give your old popster a jingle."

"OK," her voice sounded small.

He watched his daughter wobble away from him in her cheap, green, obviously painful shoes, so young, the world sweeping her up, the world ahead of her. What if she turned around? Would he be able to resist saving her? Mo forced himself to look away, to drive on home to what was waiting for him, the Tooth Fairy from Scranton, light of his life.

ELEANOR PINCHED HER GLASSES OFF and crammed them in the small green "clutch," as her mother called it, exactly what she was doing, clutching it in her icy hands. Inside its black satin interior were things her mother had tucked in: a monogrammed, lace-edged hankie, a tube of Hot Polka Dot lipstick, a small plastic comb and change for a phone call. Eleanor had added her rosary beads, one of Mother Stewart's prayer booklets, and the most recent note Mother Fitzgerald had written to her, on the back of a holy card: *My dearest Eleanor, Though our paths be different, our goal is still the same.*

Seven o'clock. Two and a half hours. Eleanor hid behind a feathery broom of potted palms before forcing herself to walk, her feet killing her, into the dimly lit ballroom. Without her glasses, she felt as if she were underwater, a pale obelisk that whole schools of exotic fish darted around, shot past. She was the only one standing, unasked. And what if she was? Asked?

What was she to do with her purse? Her feet were already numb, used to their thick sport socks and old saddle shoes. Eleanor stood there, grateful for the semidarkness, when she heard or rather felt someone ask her to dance. A tall, gangling, extra-lanky boy, he reminded her of a pinkish, faintly wet-looking daddy longlegs, wearing glasses, as she should have been. She hadn't heard him over the noise of the band, so he had poked her in the shoulder to get her attention. Now he clamped her into a wooden-legged box step, and they labored together, he blinking across her shoulder, she staring into his armpit for one whole Frank Sinatra song, then another. Clearly, they were victims of the same ballroom dance lessons. During a break in the music, her partner towered beside her, his arm soldered around her waist, happy to have zeroed in on his matching half. Eleanor freed herself, waving in what she hoped was the direction of the powder room.

"I'll be back," she shouted. Not waiting for his reaction, she limped away.

The ladies lounge was a suite of two huge, expensively fur-nished rooms, the toilets and sinks like unpleasant, functional afterthoughts. Both lemon-scented rooms glittered feverishly with pale, nervous girls, bobbing and primping in front of long, gold-flecked wall mirrors. Upon coming in, Eleanor had felt their cold, collectively dismissive glance. The velvet bow on her head condemned her. No one else wore one and her dress, she saw instantly, was last year's. For some reason, she'd imagined the bathroom would be empty, that she would be able to sit down on one of the dark green club chairs and read. Instead, she walked down to a stall at the far end marked Out of Order, went in, latched the door, nudged her shoes off and sat sideways on the toilet, her stockinged feet propped on the silver toilet-paper dispenser. She planned to say her rosary and read and reread Mother Stewart's booklet until, say, nine o'clock.

At six minutes to nine, Eleanor emerged holding her shoes and purse clipped together, and limping since her left leg and buttock had gone completely to sleep. There was a white telephone in the lobby. Her father answered on the fifth ring.

"Sentence served, Jazzie?" That made her smile. The dance wouldn't be over until twelve-thirty, yet there he would be, within ten minutes, the door to his Mustang opened for her. Mo took Eleanor out for a milkshake, while Mitzi waited at home in her red silk kimono, pleased at having so easily restored her husband's spirits. Men were simple creatures with primitive needs. She could not yet guess, waiting for Mo and Eleanor to return—where were they?—how crestfallen she would be by Eleanor's laconic answers to her inquiries: Who was there? What were the other girls wearing? Whom did she dance with? One would think she hadn't gone at all. The next morning she would search for her daughter's name in the society column ("Eleanor Stoddard, daughter of Dr. and Mrs. Morris Stoddard, wearing an all-season gold-lamé-and-white-chiffon gown . . ."), but there were just the same names that appeared week after week: Leslie Malone, Cindy Rambeault, Betsy Farasyn . . . She refused to dwell on the hypocrisy of the rich: how doors looked as if they might open but rarely did, how smiles might seem genuine but rarely were. With her usual energy, she launched into her next plan, to have Eleanor volunteer as a docent at the local art museum. She had heard that a number of girls from the wealthier families over in Atherton had begun doing that.

LACEY JENKS RAISED the black veil from her face to accept communion from the handsome, young seminary priest who had proclaimed in his homily that a girl's sins could be seen in her eyes, that God had so designed it. Coming back down the aisle of the chapel, she paused beside Eleanor to flash the double thumbs-up—old news, since she and Arthur had already had sex nine times. Still, she had waited so as not to shock Eleanor, who, if possible, was becoming ever more shockable. Now, Lacey prayed—though it was more like begging—not to be pregnant. Nine times, Arthur had talked her into letting him "pull out." "Foolproof," he had whispered. But desperate, with her period three weeks late, Lacey had read in her mom's medical book, it wasn't foolproof at all. Yesterday, Arthur had taken her to a doctor he knew for a test. Today, he would take her back for the results. All morning, during the first day of the school's annual three-day spiritual retreat, instead of contemplating God or reading from the exhausted heap of religious books the nuns trotted out every year, Lacey had written and rewritten her married name, Mrs. Arthur Webb, inked a chain of marguerite daisies, her favorite, around the edges of the letters. She'd designed bride and bridesmaid dresses, imagined a wedding along the lines of the one she had seen in *The Sound of Music*. But unshared happiness was lonely. Arthur didn't talk. He was a musician, he said, not a conversationalist. It still amazed her how easily she'd fooled her parents. At seventy-nine the Colonel could be declared legally senile, and her mother was always at the library, working overtime, or else in the house somewhere, lying down with one of her migraines. Lacey had discovered if she did her chores and her homework without complaint, her parents were so paralyzed by gratitude that they believed whatever she told them. And what she'd been telling them was she had theater rehearsals after school. Arthur waited for her on his motorcycle, took her to his apartment, afterward dropping her off by her bicycle, stashed under some pomegranate bushes near the school grounds. Handsome Father O'Malley was barking out his ass, as the Colonel liked to say. Her eyes, for she had gazed boldly up at him as he placed the dry, white host on her tongue, revealed nothing at all.

Cher Holy Noser

    I know, I know. I'm not sixteen (seize) yet, so DBM (don't be mad) at me, will explain ALL later . . .

      If I'm not at school tomorrow, pray for me. I know

how much you like to do that (pray) . . . and right now
people like me could use that (prayer).

> *Toot mon amour,*
> Mrs. Arthur Webb
> *(hee)*

AS SHE KNELT BY HER BED that night, praying for Lacey, the
Virgin Mary appeared like a bit of floating gauze in a corner of
the room by Eleanor's closet, looking somewhat like the pink-
and-blue statue in the alcove, only without any solidity. The
apparition, which she later realized also resembled Mother
Fitzgerald, lasted perhaps a second, during which Eleanor received the distant impression she had been asked—or commanded—to befriend the two queer girls, Rose and Deirdre.
Feeling foolish yet rarefied, she bowed her head before the hovering, mothlike figure and said, yes, she would obey. When she
lifted her head, it was gone.

THE NEXT MORNING, Eleanor felt as if a thick, satiny light swam
around her. She felt calm, slowed with holy purpose. At
lunchtime, in the dining hall, she took her tray of food and sat
directly across from the two girls, Rose and Deirdre. Because of
the retreat's rule of silence, Eleanor smiled, as beatifically as she
could. Suspicious, the girls glowered back, but Eleanor, undeterred, remained confident in the mission she had been given.

And lying across her bed that night, Eleanor wrote to Mother Fitzgerald (a letter she would later tear up), telling her about the vision. After brushing her teeth—since the cotillion, she had given up any other form of self-improvement—she turned out all the lights except the small yellow lamp beside her bed and waited. She didn't want to appear greedy, but she desperately needed a second vision to prove the validity of the first, which she had begun, ever so slightly, to doubt. She identified with those children who had seen Our Lady of Fatima, with young Bernadette of Lourdes. That led to Eleanor picturing herself on top of a small hill, her eyes turned heavenward, her arms uplifted, thousands of people gathered below, waiting. Was she crazy? What if this was like *The Screwtape Letters,* that C. S. Lewis book where Wormwood, or whatever the devil's name was, knew your every vanity, his job to corrupt you through diabolical temptations, semblances of virtue? Was spiritual pride tempting her to see herself as famous, chosen, special? As she knelt by her bed, squinting at the corner where she had seen Mary–Mother Fitzgerald the night before, there was a timid rap at her window, then another, then a third, more insistent. Eleanor got up and went over to see Lacey staring at her, her beautiful long hair flattened with rain, dripping about her face.

"Nors."

Eleanor could barely hear. She raised the window. "What are you doing here?" The rain became audible, wind blew coolly in. She thought she heard a motorcycle. Arthur's? It was raining hard.

"Nors. This is *très* serious. I have to go away. But I'll be back in three, maybe four days, by Monday for sure."

"Where are you going?"

"I got in a righteous argument with my parents and left a note on my bed saying I'd walked over to your house. So here's the thing. If they call, can you say I'm here and that I'll be home after school tomorrow . . ."

"If you were here, wouldn't they want to talk to you, not me?"

"Say I'm in the shower or something. Say I'm asleep. Or throwing up. The point is, I need to keep them from looking for me right away."

"Why?" Eleanor felt frightened. "Are you going somewhere with him?"

"We're going to Mexico. Just for a few days."

"Mexico?"

"Arthur knows this clinic in Tijuana where girls from his college go. It's really safe, and he's paying for the whole thing. Jesus, Eleanor. Now you'll hate me. I wish I was like you, as good as you, but I probably won't ever be. Please. Will you do that? Just tell my parents, if they call, that I'm here, staying with you?" Lacey was crying, her long hair like two shining blades down her shoulders.

"You said his motorcycle was a joke—how will you get all the way to Mexico?"

"He's been working on it all week."

When she heard that, Eleanor decided to really hate Arthur Webb. His dumb motorcycle. Dumb everything.

"OK, I'll tell them. Wait." Eleanor put her hand out the window, felt cold rain sting her wrist. "Take this?"

Lacey wiped her nose on the hem of her big sweater. "Jesus, Mary and Joseph. You've gone Catholic on me, Noser. That's OK. I already knew. I was watching you before I knocked, you looked holier than hell. Hey, my mom always says converts make the best saints." Lacey pocketed the rosary in a solemn motion. "I'll hang onto it the entire time."

SHE LOOKED FOR Lacey's bicycle on the last day of the retreat, knowing it wouldn't be there, how could it be? Still. After morning Mass, Eleanor wandered the rain-drenched school grounds, until she happened upon the nuns' plain, two-story retirement home. Behind it was a neatly kept orchard of apple trees. She sat on a patch of damp, long, yellow grass, struggling to pray, imagining instead what might be happening to her friend. Eleanor ended up going back to the empty study hall, sitting at Lacey's desk and impulsively writing a letter. In it, she recklessly declared how beautiful and perfect she believed Mother Fitzgerald to be. She did not set this letter in the usual place, upon the lectern used by the Mistress of Studies, but carried it down to the west wing of the second floor, a cloistered area where the nuns lived. The long, low-lit hall looked deserted. She ran down its length before finding the door marked M. Fitzgerald. Amazed by her own audacity, she bent down and slid the letter underneath.

At lunch, with somewhat less conviction, she sat across from Rose and Deirdre, who, this time, smiled with a combined, breathtaking trust in her. Eleanor moved her food around, worried about the letter, thinking she should write another retracting what she'd said in the first, when there was a disturbance in the hallway just outside the dining room, a breach of the retreat's heavy silence, the sound of voices conferring. Then Mother Fitzgerald, accompanied by Reverend Mother McGwynn, the Mistress General, and the school's Latin teacher, Mother Flaherty, walked in. Mother Fitzgerald looked distraught. At the familiar command of the wooden clapper, the roomful of girls rose, curtsied in the direction of their Reverend Mother and received the news that during last night's storm, there had been an accident, resulting in the premature death of one of their third-academic students. They were to proceed immediately to chapel, to pray for the soul of Lacey Ann Jenks.

Hail Mary, full of grace, the Lord is with thee, blessed art thou amongst women and blessed is the fruit of thy womb, Jesus. Holy Mary, Mother of God, pray for us sinners now and at the hour of our death, amen. Hail Mary . . .

To Mitzi's credit, she did not pry. She calmly held her daughter, then went with her to the funeral at Our Lady of Angels. Mo stayed home. All funerals, he said, especially those of children, depressed him.

At the service, Mitzi thought the parents looked terrible, as though they couldn't live through this; and indeed, Colonel Jenks would die in less than a year's time, in a car accident less than a mile from his home, due, it was said, to his failing eyesight. There was an older brother, who, with other male relatives, bore the casket, which was white and draped in a blanket of pink baby roses. Newspaper details would be scarce, though there would be the most recent yearbook photograph of Lacey. What Mitzi would later hear through friends was that Lacey had been sneaking out of the house to see her guitar instructor. Mo, hearing this from his wife, felt newly protective of Eleanor, restrictive of her whereabouts. On several heated occasions, Mitzi argued with him, heedless, for once, of his mood. If he didn't want his daughter becoming a nun, why in God's name did he suddenly insist on treating her like one? What was the matter with him, couldn't he see the child scarcely left her room anymore? But that would be weeks later, weeks after the death of Lacey Jenks.

AT THE END of her third year at the Convent of the Sacred Heart, during Prime, an awards ceremony held in the Little

Theater, Eleanor Stoddard's name was called. Again and again she was made to leave her seat and go up on the stage to be congratulated by Reverend Mother and the other nuns. She accepted medals of merit, academic certificates, even what she had once so dearly wished for, a pale blue honor ribbon. For her scholarship, in particular, for her essay on the benefits of martyrdom, which had won third place in a national Catholic Youth essay contest, for her leadership potential and community service, Eleanor Stoddard received special commendation. The following year she would be elected valedictorian and her speech, poetic and slightly scathing—not what anyone expected—would be dedicated to Lacey Jenks. But now, kneeling to receive her ribbon from Reverend Mother, applause rising respectfully behind her, Eleanor felt nothing she could identify, nothing at all.

Then, at the point when Prime usually ended, Mrs. Jenks, wearing a kelly green suit and matching hat, came forward to announce a small scholarship in her daughter's name, funded by the city's library. She wept as she spoke of the lifelong values instilled in Sacred Heart girls. Then Mrs. Jenks sat down, and the best singer in the school, Kathy Murphy, played her guitar and sang "Today, While the Blossom Still Clings to the Vine," followed by another girl Eleanor didn't know well, who had composed a villanelle about death, comparing it, in a tedious chain of verses, to a dance whose steps were ever the same.

Afterward, all four classes stood to recite a mimeographed prayer in honor of Lacey Jenks, in memory of her innocent, untried soul.

THAT SUMMER, Mo recouped his losses and was able to pay for Eleanor's first pair of contact lenses. Her braces had been removed as well, so with straight ivory teeth and wide, impassive eyes, Eleanor Stoddard seemed, over that summer, to have traded her ugly-ducklingness for some new, abject radiance. Mitzi noted, with no small relief, the disappearance of her daughter's religious articles. Though Eleanor now burned purple cones of Bombay incense in her room and wrote poetry, verse after gloomy verse wherein lovers suffered sudden, unjust deaths on the moors, or gypsies rode on horseback down white roads to the sea, disconsolate scenes all set apparently in England. Not a problem, Mo said, when Mitzi waved the poems around, having located them in her daughter's desk while Eleanor was away at an exclusive girls camp in Lake Tahoe, and Mitzi'd begun redecorating her room in a French Provincial theme. A phase, he said. No doubt she was copying the stuff out of some book somewhere; it seemed pretty sophisticated; he couldn't make head nor tail of it. Though he did remember writing some pretty sour material when he was trying to get over his first girlfriend's leaving him. Death and heartbreak, he reminded Mitzi, throw you the hardest.

Cecilia Mornay, the daughter of a high government official

in Haiti, sat in a yellow silk damask chair, a cup of tea balanced on her lap, gazing up at the senior girl introduced by Mother Fitzgerald as her Angel. The fall tea, as always, was held in the immaculately appointed front parlor and, up to this point, Eleanor had successfully avoided looking at Mother Fitzgerald. Her letter, shot under the nun's door, with its reckless avowal of passion, had never been acknowledged. There had been no reply, the long summer had ensued and now, Eleanor thought to herself, hearing Mother Fitzgerald prattle on about the school's soccer and tennis teams, gesturing with familiar, ruddy, athletic movements, how pathetically jolly, how ignorant. How could she have thought this nun graceful or sensitive, attached hope or perfection to her? The spell was broken, a spell much like that cast by the Blessed Virgin over innocence. What she could not know was how hungrily her letter had been received, how Mother Fitzgerald had, after many written and discarded replies, expressions of love returned in kind, added Eleanor's crie de coeur to all the others she had saved from various girls, and taken them downstairs to the basement incinerator. With a prayer that she be forever spared wanting to be loved in such deplorable ways, Mother Fitzgerald pitched the letters, bound together, cries of love identical and shallow in each girl's heart, the same in her own, into the incinerator's constant, dirty fire.

AFTER SOME WEEKS, Cecilia Mornay found herself content, adjusting to this newest school. She was popular with the other

girls and felt some guilt that she no longer relied upon Eleanor
Stoddard, avoided her anyway, always so serious and worse,
openly critical of the one person Cecilia liked best, Mother
Fitzgerald. As her soccer team's captain, Cecilia excelled, in
part to see the nun's face flush with pleasure, to hear her ring-
ing shouts of triumph. Only recently they had begun exchang-
ing small notes handwritten in French, Cecilia's first language.
Eleanor showed no interest in athletics; her attitudes were
those of a nihilist, a nonparticipant, an unsmiling intellectual,
all of which Cecilia found abhorrent and unappealing. Eleanor
commanded respect, certain cold attributes of leadership and
realms of knowledge were hers, but Cecilia felt unsettled in her
presence. Back home in Haiti, her mother would explain such
a sensation by saying a ghost walked with that one, you can be
sure.

> *Queen of Angels*
> *Of Martyrs*
> *Of Virgins*
> *Of Peace*
> *Of Sinners and Saints*
> *Singular Vessel,*
> *Save us.*

Three days after the motorcycle accident, Eleanor knelt before the Virgin. When at last she stood up, she saw Lacey Jenks

sitting beside the statue. Neatly dressed in her school uniform, her hair darkened, glittering with rain. On her lap was a white index card with blurred red lettering Eleanor could not decipher. That night, waking up in her bed, Eleanor thought she saw Lacey, haloed in silver mist, moving toward the window. And for what would prove to be the last time, during Mass the following morning, Eleanor would see her dead friend, floating and naked, as if on her stomach, above the handsome but obstinate Father O'Malley, her fingers splayed in a V above his head. She smiled, tenderly and without judgment, before her features were washed over by a fierce, impenetrable gaze, a look Eleanor Stoddard began, without awareness, to reflect, drawing to herself all who desired to see what it was that overturned human love, what mystery it was that so crowned the heart with cold braided thorns, one strand glory, the other a blind, perdurable grace.

Virgin Blue

Nora met Evan when she was eighteen and he was twenty-five. They lived in a toolshed with an indigent's view of the sea, haunting the periphery of Santa Barbara's wealthy community in a yellow 1949 Cadillac named the Canary. They'd met during a guerrilla theater performance when Nora, lobbing balloons of fake blood against the steps of the downtown Bank of America, nailed, by accident or destiny, Evan's bare feet. He told her he owned a place near the university called The Dirty Bookstore. It was the size of a millionaire's walk-in closet, and while Evan knelt on a paisley cushion outside the store, concentrating on a Japanese board game calling for strategically imperceptible movements of smooth black and white stones, The Dirty Bookstore's clients, older men, slouched past, trench coats belted, hats brimmed low. Nora once asked if there wasn't a costume shop around the corner that rented out the hats and trench coats. Paranoid about jail, Evan warned and rewarned his sole employee, a Vietnam vet named Lurch, not to sell to anyone under twenty-one, her for instance, he'd point out Nora, bundled in her Navy peacoat, black kohl snaked around her eyes, a shag haircut like Jane Fonda's in *Klute*. Evan enrolled in Russian language courses at the university and acted in most of their theater productions; in every play there seemed to be a part for a short conniver, a nasty jester. Turning nineteen, Nora was boiling over or broody, depending on the hour, with discontent. Evan had turned out to be much less than the local legend she had initially been enthralled by. He was fading local color, and Nora was putting up with him now, that's how she thought of it, putting up with, which sounded and felt wife-ish. His compulsive infidelities with costumers and prop girls along with his stock perversity, smacking Nora across her "cute, white ass" with a leather strap, were not, she reasoned, in her finest interest. Although living with Evan fixed the enemy as a perverse little man outside herself, still, her struggle for worth was perpetual, so chronic it verged on habit. Until now. Until this play she'd gotten a part in. Until Kellen. Until the part of Pam, a gabby British housewife who blew onstage in a rayon slip, chain-smoking and grousing about her varicosed calves. But no matter. Nora was in love, the true kind which made her hope to exceed herself. She'd given up trying to locate an identity—a consistent self—and felt more like a vertical blank surface reflecting whatever was set before it, and now, with Kellen as her director, Nora, who only faintly aspired to be an actress, awaited an opportunity to shine him blindingly back to himself.

THE PLAY CONCERNED a middle-class British couple whose daughter, Faith, renamed Joe Egg by the father in a moment's cruelty—*look at her, will you, she's just sitting around like Joe Egg*—had cerebral palsy. The couple's marriage suffers, the child suffers, hills and heaps of suffering all around—it was really a very grim play—with Kellen both director and mixed-up father. No one in the cast, five altogether, minded much, since he was so personable. Kellen was the first perfect person Nora had ever met—a contagion of joy poured off him, an ecumenical ledger of virtues and unassailable goodnesses. He was only twenty, a year older than Nora, and what she wanted was to so cunningly play herself that he would fall in love with her, which meant falling more deeply in love with himself, the sort of trick Nora was best at. To that end, she thought of Park Haven, where she had worked once. (Despite its infusion of private monies and chilly, Italianate landscaping, Park Haven was little more than an institution, a storage bin. Inside, the staff padded about on chumpy white shoes; even the furniture looked clinically prescribed, like buttons of aspirin.) After the cast's first read-through, when Kellen asked what any of them knew about cerebral palsy, Nora confessed nothing. She waited until everyone left before suggesting to him that the five of them visit Park Haven so the play would be more authentic, more true to life.

In the middle of what Howard, Nora's stage husband, referred to as the "geek-gawk," Kellen befriended Joe Kerr, a young man writing his autobiography. Otherwise, the group visit had gone poorly. Once inside the vestibule of Park Haven, four of them—Nora, Marcia, Howard and Audrey—stood like a pasted-up lump of flesh, hinged together by the off-kilter British accents they were supposed to practice until the play opened. They were there to observe disability, chat up victims in wheelchairs, children afflicted with spastic paralysis (an old word, a staff nurse informed them, even "cerebral palsy" a garbage-can term, sweeping into it anyone whose brain injury affected muscle control). Nora told no one she had worked one week in Park Haven's kitchen before being fired for shoving a blue waxed box of Snowcap lard in her purse—a joke for Evan. Just as she had been then, Nora was disquieted by Park Haven's bland Lutheran charmlessness, the linoleum's milky repellent sheen. In the lobby, floor-to-ceiling glass allowed a view of ponderosa pine, though even these, in their regimented rows, looked sinister and staged. So much fastidious polish suggested discouragement, erasures of quirk, the negating of distinctive wallows and spikes of personality. Color brochures, fanned out beside a bird-of-paradise arrangement on the receptionist's desk, called Park Haven home to sixty-five residents, clearly routed there by way of exceedingly well-to-do relatives.

"Shouldn't we be interviewing," Howard whispered to Nora, "jotting down specifics of the disease, that sort of thing—some visible passport of purpose?"—he actually said that. Howard was an English major who "dabbled" in dramatics, wore polka-dot bow ties and spoke like Nora didn't know what, a goofy professor. Holding, ticketlike, their Park Haven brochures, Nora, Howard, Marcia and Audrey straggled over to the furniture in the lobby, seated themselves on Scandinavian chairs with nubbly, lime green cushions. It was noon, with cafeteria noise floating down the hall, carrying with it a faint, pernicious smell of cabbage and boiled meat. With the guilt of the able-bodied, they watched Kellen lope up the hall from the cafeteria, six or seven children in wheelchairs surging around him. Audrey, the high school senior who played Joe Egg, mostly by slumping in her wheelchair and feigning an occasional rough seizure, gnawed her nails and muttered, "Christ on a crutch." Howard, who on the drive back to the theater would repeat "poor buggers" numerous times as he stared glumly out the car window, finagled his face into a bright expression, utterly failing to disguise his distress at seeing such mangled bits, queerly knobbed birds of humanity. Only Marcia, who played Kellen's wife, seemed calm and unperturbed, kneeling like a relief worker to talk to several children at once. Nora worriedly looked about for the mean woman who had caught her stealing the lard, a Mrs. Peacock (who, it turned out, had been fired herself). And Kellen, displaying wholesome exuberance, slung his guitar off one broad shoulder, dropped cross-legged to the floor and with children clustered in glinting metal nests all around him, began to sing. More children came wheeling down from various hallways while the staff, arms crossed, approving, hovered in the background—"quite the nursery scrim," Howard's peevish comment.

"They adored you," Marcia said, casting a worshipful glance of her own at Kellen as they all drove back to the theater. It was clear she hoped being his stage wife might work some alchemical influence, though everyone believed Kellen to be fatally besotted with Audrey's older sister, a cold dash of water named Yvette.

"Right-o," said Howard in his wincingly stillborn Cockney. "Obviously a Pied Piper." Still, their rehearsal that evening had unexpected energy. Audrey modeled her posture after a little girl she'd seen at Park Haven, and they all felt a more united sympathy for their characters, even for the ethically daft father, bent on murdering his daughter to shore up his marriage. The thing, said Kellen, was to keep improving their accents, which, he hated to say it, were atrocious.

Two days later, Kellen took Nora with him to Park Haven to visit Joe Kerr. They were in Kellen's green VW bug, the dash heaped with wilted blue lupine and California poppy. Nora wore her newest thrift-store finds, a parochial school blouse and vintage circle skirt, handpainted labial pink with sudsy palm trees and a golden-eyed jaguar prowling the dirty hem. Kellen wore a blue workman's shirt, jeans, leather sandals, a blue headband knotted around his long, honey-brown hair. Nora had never known anyone so handsome, unaffected, kind. *Solar exhuberance,* she put down in her journal, squiggling blue roses around his name, then scratching the whole thing out. Maybe certain people sieved through language and were lost. Like the standard defense for a joke no one laughed at—you had to be there—you had to be in Kellen's presence to believe in unscathed happiness. It was as if he had never been harmed, which is to say never born, and how could that be, didn't everyone protect themselves by perfecting the subtler, meaner skills of growing up?

IN THE ROOM he shared with a nine-year-old boy named Stigler, Joe Kerr had a metal desk and, on top of the desk, a manual typewriter. Against the wall was a stack of pink bakery boxes, holding, Joe said, his unfinished autobiography. While they waited for Dolores, his girlfriend, Joe demonstrated how he typed, clamping a pencil between his teeth, tapping each key. It took up to an hour to roll a piece of paper in and more than an hour, sometimes two, to write one page. He became enraged, he told them, when his thoughts shot past what his body could do. As Joseph Kerr II, he was the oldest son of a tool-and-die manufacturer in Chicago. His first five years were spent on the second floor of the family mansion in Winnetka, until his parents were advised it would be best for everyone, particularly Joe, if he were sent here. Joe arched back his neck, laughing. "I cramped their style. Here's the chapter I'm writing now. About Dolores. I call it 'Fairy Tale.' It starts with how she was dumped into a state hospital in Brooklyn, how her mother was told to take her to an institution, 'forget you had her, you've got other mouths to feed.' Then—here's the fairy-tale part—last year, some cousin no one knew about died and left money so Dolores could go to a private home. Where she met me. Here she comes now. Hey. Dolores. Remember me telling you about these guys, the ones doing the play? You do? OK." He looked at Nora. "Would you mind? Dolores needs the bathroom. It's down the hall to the right. Otherwise we have to call the staff nurse, and that can take forever."

Dolores was surprisingly heavy to push, and Nora, who had been told the week before at the public health clinic that she had a heart murmur, maneuvered the wheelchair into the ladies room, where she rolled down Dolores' large white cotton underpants, scooted her onto the toilet, waited, wiped her front and back, seesawed her underwear back up around her waist, hefted her back into the wheelchair, stuffed with rolled towels, clumps of clothing, cheap decorator pillows. Dolores was a big girl with lank, carob-brown hair, skinny, mink-colored eyes, thick glasses galaxied with dandruff, newsprint-colored skin, lips bunchy and chapped. Besides being big, Dolores was wrenchingly plain, so it was with a lurch of near-infatuation that Nora saw Dolores' pubic hair, a black, glossy nest between the two forked branches of her legs. Nora was still seeing it, angling the wheelchair backwards, pushing out the door, breathless from her heart, still in love with that starry nest when she found Joe, in his Day-Glo wheelchair, waiting beside Kellen, who came right over to help her.

"Hey Nora. Joe says he's never been to the beach. Neither has Dolores. No one's ever taken them out of this place, so I just asked to borrow one of Park Haven's vans. Come with us tomorrow. I want you with us."

Evan had been nagging at her for weeks to make a skinflick, a blue movie for some people he'd met in L.A. "Five hundred dollars for something you've done—hell, we've done—hundreds of times, Nora."

"Not in front of the world. Not in front of strangers."

"You're an actress. What's the difference?"

Five hundred dollars—it would take months of waitressing and cleaning houses to save up that kind of money. She could take it and split for Mendocino. Mt. Shasta. According to Evan, his last girlfriend, who had flown over from London to study Japanese calligraphy and Gestalt therapy, had made enough to pay her way, first class, to India.

"I have an appointment to meet with two producers down in Burbank tomorrow. Just to talk. You don't have to say anything. Or do anything. Just come with me."

As far as she could throw a stick, Nora didn't trust him. They'd get there and it would all be different from what he'd said. He'd convince her things were safe, and when his promises got her going, he'd make her do whatever he wanted. Still. Five hundred dollars.

"I can't. I'm going with some friends to the beach tomorrow. If you want, I'll think about it."

"What's to think? What are you getting paid to do that play of yours?"

"Nothing. It's art."

"Exactly. Well, guess what? You can make art and get paid. You've got a beautiful ass, Nora."

"What's that supposed to mean?"

"It means I'm sick and twisted, the way you like me best." Evan dragged her down to the grimy mattress that didn't have sheets or pillows, just two old sleeping bags, the teeth so worn they didn't zip together anymore. When he'd first brought her to the toolshed, Nora had been reading Dostoyevsky's *Crime and Punishment*. Evan, she thought, bore an uncanny resemblance to the murderer Raskolnikov, the ex-student in his filthy rags, brilliant, paranoid, repulsively handsome, full of mad plots. But Evan's filth had turned boring. And the literary depth had never existed, she had invented it.

Splitting a joint with Evan, Nora wound up talking about Joe, how she'd helped Dolores in the bathroom, almost bragging she'd wiped somebody's ass for them (Kellen was higher caliber, he wouldn't see that as anything special, just another joyful opportunity). She was spacing out on Kellen, on the idea that a person of superior virtue could, unwittingly, make others feel inferior and thus find himself both resented and revered, when Evan started talking about one of his aunts back east who had had cerebral palsy, how his mother used to make him go with her on holidays to visit Aunt Margaret. Years later, he'd learned what a nightmare the state hospital had been for his aunt: how Margaret, with her bright mind, brighter than most, had been mixed in with imbeciles, hydroencephalics, people who ate their own feces; how three or four of them would be tossed like kittens into this big, high-sided box for what was called socialization, left in there all day, no matter what. Fascists.

"What happened?"

"To my aunt? Starved herself. It took her years to die."

NORA COULD NOT BELIEVE how long it took to get Joe and Dolores out of Park Haven, into the pale blue van and down to the beach. Half the day. The sand, where she'd poured a milk carton of seawater over it, shone like an uneven police badge. Dolores' wheelchair was parked right off the end of a plywood board Kellen had slapped over the sand, end over end, like a thick, giant's playing card.

At first, Dolores, her face hidden under a puckered white canvas hat patriotically sprigged with tiny red flags, had been terrified by the crashing of the waves; her hypersensitive startle reflexes caused her arms and legs to shoot wildly about. Now she was quiet, her head lolling to one side, the wheelchair angled so she could see the water. Joe sat nearby in a sort of crooked W, his knees splayed beneath him. He wore Stigler's black swim trunks, which were too small, and his white, extremely skinny chest and back were stippled with a bumpy red rash. Kellen, sitting nearby, had undressed Joe in the van, carried and set him down before helping Nora bring Dolores down. Nora sat unlacing Dolores' grimy tennis shoes, tugging them off, massaging each foot, working the flat arch, the soft heel, Dolores' sallow feet set loose from their canvas houses with the spoiled grey tongues. Squinting at Kellen through her gold, swan-shaped sunglasses, she imagined that, like Dolores, she had never heard the sea's low, mournful chop or seen its weary-ing surface.

Joe was exhuberant, windblown, hoarse from shouting over the moving green hills of the sea. He shouted to Kellen to carry him down to the water. Dolores, her head to one side, smiled without discernment, seeming to endlessly approve of anything Joe did. For this alone, Nora thought, Joe would be wild for her. Dolores was, he insisted, clever, slyly funny, though Nora had seen only the constant, almost creepy smile. Her cerebral palsy, he'd explained on the short drive to the beach, was much worse than his. She had hypotonicity, or floppiness of the muscles, which meant she had trouble speaking, feeding herself, even using her hands. In her wheelchair, propped into a sitting posi-tion with rolled towels and pillows stuffed around her, a leather strap around her waist, she resembled a plump, broken-necked sparrow. Joe had an opposite affliction, hypertonicity, contrac-tion of the muscles, so that he became rigid, spastic, hands splaying, his neck, sometimes his whole back arching back-wards, a raw, splitting bow. Dolores "talked," using subtle eye movements or mucus-tinged sounds, the meanings of which

mostly escaped Nora, although Joe, whose own speech was labored and sometimes slurry, always knew what she wanted. In
her big grocer-green housecoat, Dolores reminded Nora of an
old, worn pot holder, square and limp. Before they'd left Park
Haven that morning, she'd helped her on and off the toilet,
changing the sanitary pad, soaked dark red, that someone else
had put on backwards and upside down.

"Where's my old lady?" Joe rolled his body over and over
across the sand, until, on his back, he was looking boldly up
Dolores' parted legs. On all fours, he crept around her wheelchair, swinging his head as if stalking prey, before nibbling at
one of her puffy white ankles. Dolores grinned until drool fell
from both sides of her mouth. Nora reached up with the edge
of a beach towel to wipe it away.

"Come on, buddy, let's hit the waves." Cradling Joe in his
arms, Kellen smiled down at Nora. "Cool shades, Nora."

All the better to hide, she thought. I don't want God's perfect likeness seeing me, damn it. She turned away and spoke to
Dolores.

"You OK, hon? Want anything from the van? A blanket?
Another towel? You warm enough?"

Dolores made a garbling sound Nora decided meant she
was fine.

"Look Dolores. Far out. Joe's got Kellen carrying him like a
sack of potatoes straight into the sea. I'm going to run down
there and find some seashells for you. Be right back."

After a minute or so in the water, Joe's skin was marbled from cold, his teeth smacking together, so Nora and Kellen worked fast to get him up to the van in the parking lot. They went back to get Dolores, whose hat had blown off and gone pinwheeling down the beach. In her shirt pocket, Nora had a sand dollar, black mussels shiny as beetles' backs, even a channeled whelk to put in Dolores' room, on her dresser. Dolores shared a room with a woman named LaVerne, who sat in bed watching cartoons, shouting the same phrases over and over—"Good Dad, Good Dad, Good Dad," or "Poddy, Momma, Poddy Momma." Echolalia, one of the staff nurses called it. LaVerne could repeat a phrase for hours on end. A thing like echolalia would drive Nora out of her mind. LaVerne's half of the room was loaded with religious objects, calendars, needlework sayings (Be still and know I am God), crosses wrapped with plastic flowers. Dolores had a different worship going on her side. Beatles posters, Beatles figurines, biographies, paperweights, even a Yellow Submarine wall clock.

THE FOUR OF THEM settled into the van, the heater roaring out uneven patches of heat. Kellen, who had started a conversation, was in the driver's seat, Joe beside him. Nora and Dolores were in the back. Double date, thought Nora.

"Joe, I'm serious, man. Do you maybe want to take Dolores to a nice restaurant? How about the zoo? A movie? The

Museum of Natural History? I'm pretty sure we can get the van whenever we want. What would you like to do next time?"

Joe was bundled up in three beach towels; his face, splotched and red, poked out like a hatchet.

"Get it on with my old lady."

"What?" Kellen looked blank.

"Screw our brains out."

Dolores let out an insane giggle, a goosey shriek.

"Dolores knows what I mean. At Park, it's easier on them if we have no feelings. Of the sexual type. They keep the men and women separated. It's discrimination."

Kellen turned around. "That so, Dolores?"

She made a sound Nora easily interpreted as yes. With all Joe's horsing around, Nora had never once imagined them having sex. Fucking. How would they? Why would they want to?

Kellen was looking at her, waiting for help.

"A motel?" She said it so fast it sounded sleazy. It made her think of Evan's pornography.

"Exactly. This is what, Saturday? I'll tell Mrs. Whoosit, the lady at the front desk, that the four of us are going to dinner Monday night, maybe a movie. Instead, we'll go to a motel."

"An orgy?" Joe's wet hair spiked out in black tufts from his beach towel as he head-butted the dashboard. Nora imagined plugging Joe and Dolores together, the way she used to mate her stuffed animals, wrapping plush arms around each other, pressing noses to kiss. Later, when she sat with Kellen on the steps outside the theater, waiting for Marcia and Howard, Kellen told her what Joe had said—that Dolores had such a crush on her physical therapist in New York, she'd had orgasms in her dreams, though she didn't know what orgasms were, and Joe had to tell her.

"You mean Joe got to tell her. He would love explaining that. Do you think they're virgins?"

"What else, given where they live? Treated like they've been spayed."

"I feel dumb."

"Why?"

"I kind of thought of them that way. Spayed. That's how I thought of them."

"Nora. How many people do you really know with cerebral palsy?"

"Two. Joe and Dolores."

"So how much could either one of us possibly know about it? Joe says he's got quite a stash of pornography. He's been obsessed with sex for years now."

Lucky Dolores. Nora wondered if any of it came from Evan's Dirty Bookstore.

"OK IF I USE this washcloth? Look at this shit, will you? I've had it ages. I can't believe I actually used to wear this crapola. Argh. Here's my old eyelash curler, we'll skip that, tweezers, skip those too. Here's something possibly useful—lipsticks, mascara. Want music, Dolores?" Nora flipped the radio on, hoping it was OK with LaVerne, strapped into bed wearing an old football jersey and men's pajama bottoms, her eyes shut as if she were asleep. Nora plunked on the edge of the bed, her feet hooking for stability into the wheelchair spokes, and circled Dolores' face with the damp washcloth. She put the makeup on, brushed out Dolores' sparse ponytail, turned and reached into her backpack. "I picked this up (she did not say steal, who knew Dolores' morals?) in a head shop on State Street; it's got these little mirrors sewn into the fabric—cool, huh?—it's from India." Nora rolled the red scarf, knotted it around Dolores' forehead. "Okeydoke. Whoops, almost forgot the patchouli. Très seductive stuff." After splotching oil behind Dolores' ears, Nora reached into her backpack and dragged out a velvet dress, tie-dyed green and deep blue with long, polleny streaks of yellow. As Nora helped put the dress on, right arm first, head, then left arm, Dolores made an unmistakable moan of pleasure.

With the velvet bunched up so it wouldn't drag under the wheels, Dolores used her feet, the way she always did, to push her wheelchair toward Joe, waiting with Kellen by the front door. As she got close, he started rocking his orange wheelchair, pounding his fists on the padded arms. He had showered, his black hair was still damp, a bit of bloodied white tissue stuck to his freshly shaved chin. He wore jeans and a work shirt. Kellen's. He had a blue suede headband on. Kellen's.

"Creep," Dolores managed to say. Her fake-tortoiseshell glasses were scotchtaped on one side, the one small blight on her face, thought Nora.

THERE WERE TWO queen-sized beds, each with a thin, coral bedspread. All four of them stared at the cheaply framed pictures over each bed, one a velvet paint-by-number of a dark-skinned girl in a provocative, off-the-shoulder blouse, the other an ocean sunset with a seagull (housefly, Joe said) battering across a permanently aggrieved horizon.

"Motel art," said Kellen, causing Dolores to pitch forward with laughter.

"Wine!" shouted Joe. Kellen uncorked the bottle, poured wine into four plastic cups. Nora fussed, switching on the two bedside lamps, turning off the harsh overhead light, drawing shut the yellow, plastic-lined drapes, turning on the heater and, mostly from habit, sticking two ashtrays and a wrapped soap bar into her purse. Then she sat by Dolores, poked a straw into her mouth, held the cup. Joe angled his head down to the cup on the nightstand and sucked noisily from his straw. "Hold your horses," Kellen laughed. "Don't go getting blasted."

"Blasted!" shouted Joe, kicking at the nightstand. Nora worried he got too excited. What if he had a fit, didn't he have those sometimes? And with Dolores so torpid, you worried the other direction, that she might quit breathing.

Nora poured herself another glass of wine. Maybe she

should be the one getting blasted. "This place smells like a head shop," she said. "It's the patchouli," she waved her cup. "Huzzah!"

"Dolores wants a separate bed." Joe's head was jerking to one side, his neck winging back, the bit of Kleenex still stuck to his chin.

Kellen looked perplexed. "Who's sleeping?"

Dolores hit her hand against her chest, rocked around and around in a small, tight circle. Oh, thought Nora. They're nervous. They're virgins.

She rolled Dolores into the green-tiled bathroom to pee. Afterward, when Kellen took Joe into the bathroom, Nora helped Dolores into the bed farthest from the door, where she lay faceup in Nora's dress, arms stiff along her sides, eyes blinking.

"You look great, Dolores." Actually, she looked ready to cry. Nora picked the glasses off, set them on the nightstand. "What's to see? Want help with the dress? Yes? OK. Arms up. Alley-oop." Nora unhooked the dingy bra, slipped it off Dolores' breasts, which were big-nippled and creamy, with wavy flags of hair, like seaweed, under Dolores's arms. "Underwear too? The works?"

Just then the bathroom door crashed open. Joe sailed out in his wheelchair, naked, except for Kellen's blue headband. *Do-lo-reys* . . . he sang out. *Do-lo-reys* . . . Before she could look away, Nora saw his erection, like a long white piano key.

Under the coral covers, Dolores rolled her body in a low wave.

WITH THE WINDOWS of the van cranked down, Nora and Kellen sat awhile, unsure what to do. Nora stared at the neon blue sign, Sea Breeze Motel, making new words out of the letters. SEAR BREAST TOE TEAM BRAT . . .

"Hungry, Nora?"

"No, I keep picturing one of them, both of them, falling out of bed."

"I'm worried about the wine. Joe was pretty hammered."

"No, the wine was great, it made them both feel really adult. Me, too."

"Wine made you feel adult?"

"Just kidding. I don't know what I'm saying. What time is it?"

"Joe asked for two hours, right? Wow. An hour and fifty minutes to go."

"Hey, Kellen. What did you say during yesterday's rehearsal—about dialogue?"

"Dialogue is the last thing that happens between two people. That's not original by the way. I read it somewhere."

"That's OK. It's still true. Everything happens before we speak."

They walked, not far from the motel, down a sandy embankment swollen thick with spears of ice plant, until they came to a railroad track, its rails like wet, pitted lines of silver.

There were trees, tamarisks, along either side, and a cool wind blew off the ocean as Kellen and Nora balanced on opposite rails, one foot ahead of the other, heel-toe, heel-toe, arms outstretched, keeping even with each other. When they came to a clearing beyond the trees, Kellen ran easily up a steep, rocky slope and stood facing the sea. Nora stepped off the rail, anxious about her heart though she knew that was silly, her heart was perfectly fine. Catching her breath, looking up at him, she saw something she would try, later, to draw in her journal before ripping out the page. She would sketch a tall young man standing on a sandy bluff overlooking the sea, a poet-prince, his long brown hair buffeting around his shoulders. She could not capture the dangerous purity, the ominous innocence, standing as if on an otherworldly threshold, something she would later see as a premonition she had denied. Just as her heart began to hurt from the sight of him, Kellen turned and called down to her, held out his hand to bring her up the last shifting steps to the hilltop with its inky tussocks of beach grass. They faced the sea, her hand caught inside his, in the simplest way.

Two hours later, when there was no response to Nora's gentle knock, Kellen turned the motel key. They found Dolores and Joe on the floor between the two beds, in a tangle of blankets, asleep in each other's arms.

SINCE KELLEN WAS OVER an hour late, Marcia, like the pick-up-the-pieces wife in *Joe Egg* suggested they just do a line run-through. Nora repeated the one thing she knew, that Kellen was supposed to have been back from Los Angeles, where he'd gone to visit his mother. The four of them sat on the black-painted floor of the stage, ditching their accents, even Howard, who had a pawky head cold and kept honking into his monogrammed handkerchief. Audrey was sulking, so Marcia gave her Kellen's part, a mistake, as this involved a three-page monologue which Audrey trawled through with dogged apathy. When the offstage phone rang, Howard leapt at the excuse to exit such misery, then came back with ridiculous news, something about a kid in a Corvette running a stoplight at seventy miles an hour, hitting Kellen's green Volkswagen.

SHE WALKED AROUND the north wing of Park Haven, guessed which window, raised the sash, stuck her head in.

"Joe? Can I come in? It's me."

He was there, in the dark. Stigler's bed was empty. A radio was playing.

"Sure. Kellen with you?"

She could not answer. Not yet. "Hey, Joey. Let me get into bed with you a minute, would you?"

The need to be held, the hunger to be naked. Nora took her dress off, the green and blue one, slipped off her sandals, her underpants.

She held his skinny, stiff, trembling body. He told her about that night with Dolores, how she let him touch her, then got afraid so they started laughing, rolled off the bed, fell asleep holding each other. "Dolores and I were kind of hoping you and Kellen could take us to that place again. That motel? You should see how Dolores craves me now. She's all over me."

Nora felt his erection against her thigh. She ran her hands along his arms, his chest, reaching up to his face, his hair, her fingers touching the blue headband.

"It's all right," she said, moving a little, putting him inside her. "This is good. Kellen's here."

"Dolores too?"

"Yes." Which made Nora see all three of them in some blue, choppy movie, one bed for Joe and Dolores, one just for her. After he cried out, Nora rested her head on his white, racing chest and heard something like pain, the roaring of the sea.

The Case of the
Disappearing Ingenue

"My, I'm glad you came, Nancy!" Bess exclaimed. "George has been frightfully worried that something might have happened to you."

"To me! What an idea!" Nancy laughed it off.

"I worry every minute that you'll get into real danger," George confessed.

"Why, I've been so good lately, it hurts," Nancy replied.

—from *The Clue of the Velvet Mask: A Nancy Drew Mystery*

by CAROLYN KEENE

Eleanor Luther, once known to her Isabella Street neighbors as "Kit" (for "Kitten"), and to the various small children of Isabella and Thayer Streets as "Moo" or "Mooser," happened, while dusting her husband's nightstand, upon a terrible clue. Like the miniature key given by Bluebeard to his newest and most naive wife—"My palace is yours, dearest, but for one small door"—Eleanor plonked down on the just-stripped bed to read lyrics dashed out in Neil's spidery, introverted hand:

Your smile is like sunlight
Your love is all mine
Your eyes blue magic
Your blonde hair divine . . .

Oh fudge, thought Eleanor. Oh rot. She tried to squeeze herself, like a long, ugly foot, into the glass slipper of those soppy lyrics, but catching her woesome reflection in the full-length mirror, conceded not, surely not. Neil's other symptoms—the custom-made Italian suit, his morning isometrics, Friday's rock 'n' roll night (when she was deliberately kept in the dark as to his whereabouts until he returned at 2 A.M.), the sexual lethargy governing their bed—these could be overlooked, excuses could be made, but wasn't a love song evidence hard and undismissable as a rock? Eleanor jabbed the note back into the paperback book it had dropped out of (*The Milagro Beanfield War*), and resumed cleaning, switching on the vacuum that had once belonged to Neil's grandmother, heavy as a torpedo, roaring like hell's oven, and, for all its sound and fury, picking up very little. Neil's miserly streak was another of the many things they argued over subliminally. As a housekeeper, Eleanor balked and no doubt this was why—you risked uncovering something. If Neil was having an affair, why ever should she know?

Eleanor Stoddard met Neil Luther eight years before, when she was a Congregational minister's secretary, and he had loped into the church office to ask directions. She had never met anyone so handsome (people regularly mistook him for Clint Eastwood), so reckless, so physically impulsive. Eleanor judged herself ordinary as salt, too methodical, which of course drew her to men who were passionate, men unafraid of being boys. When their first date consisted of sitting beside the closed casket of a stranger in a third-rate Chicago funeral home, sole mourners besides a blue marlin, preserved and mounted on the wall behind them, when they first lay in her bed together and he whispered, "You look weird in the dark," Eleanor understood she had met the father of her future children. Child.

Little Marylou, six, was on schedule with other little girls in the tidy curriculum of a Midwestern suburb. Tumbling, gymnastics, ice-skating, ballet, and this week, Eleanor would begin chauffeuring her daughter to horse stables in nearby Morton Grove. Gymnastics daunted Eleanor, ice-skating vexed her, she disliked being huddled near the ice with the rest of the mothers in their mauve and teal parkas, inert as pillows. And ballet, with its potbellied, insect-legged girls, wobbling and starved, made Eleanor so restless, she wound up auditioning for the Wilmette Community Theater's next play, *Picnic,* landing Kim Novak's part, Madge, playing opposite a college dropout named Buzz Needles, who told long, filthy jokes and looked nothing like William Holden. On opening night, Neil's whole family (large, Catholic and boistrous) turned out, and her parents shipped a lei from Hawaii made of anthuriums, red, waxy, heart-shaped flowers with mortifyingly erect, bright yellow stamens that gave Buzz grist for a hundred terrible jokes. Eleanor's three brothers-in-law complimented her (the youngest, who drew her name for Christmas several weeks later, would give her a highly suggestive peignoir set), but then the play was—poof!—over, with Eleanor tucked back in her house, gaining weight, or else driving Marylou around in the ancient Mercedes Neil had brought home on New Year's Eve. She and Marylou had been down with Chinese flu, so Neil had a friend drive him to the Polish section of Chicago, where he paid cash for something he admitted to buying, literally, and in a state of intoxication, in the dark. It had a butterscotch leather interior, a sunroof that leaked, and a hole in the floorboard the perfect size and shape of a meat-loaf pan. The car stalled regularly, floating like a broken toy over to various curbs, but Eleanor noticed that when she drove it, male drivers tended to ogle and wink at her. When she drove their old station wagon, Blue Buster, no one ogled, no one winked. They were too busy getting out of the way.

The time would come when Eleanor Luther would speculate on the fateful coincidence of reading Nancy Drew mysteries aloud to Marylou that winter. In the wake of her encounter with Richard Bailey, it would seem as if events were not random, things in life were paired, like binary elements, and when a third element was introduced, combustion, followed by an incendiary fate, was altogether possible. Marylou and horses. Eleanor and Nancy Drew. Neil and Eleanor. Neil and his big blond secret. Eleanor and Richard Bailey. Richard Bailey and the murdered heiress to the Brach candy fortune. Poor Helen Brach. Like Madge in *Picnic,* or herself on Isabella Street, yet another ingenue, but with oodles, scads, electrifying heaps of money. If ingenues tended to gravitate to nefarious or otherwise exciting persons, then a wealthy (and aging) ingenue would surely be a magnet for villains.

If A (Helen Brach) equals B (villain magnet), and
B (magnet) equals C (R. Bailey), then
A (Brach) equals (murdered by villain, Bailey).

It was, in Eleanor's mind, a lopsided but still dazzling, syllogism.

Eleanor and her neighbor, Audrey Stanhope, had signed their daughters up for equitation class. Basic schooling. With the other mothers, they perched on metal bleachers in the indoor arena, watching their little darlings in black helmets, black boots, white shirts and tan breeches, rumps like underripe apricots bouncing against the saddles, backs straight as xylophones, riding crops in hand. There seemed to be a lot of sitting atop standing animals, waiting for what, Eleanor couldn't say, but the children looked dear, like stick figures atop great lagging beasts, brutes misshapen and sickle-backed, with dropped bellies, knobby hocks and short necks, kennel dogs with long legs, hammerheads, pony mongrels. That first day, Eleanor found herself watching a short man in old-fashioned jodphurs, standing by the door leading to the barns and arguing with one of the foreign stable hands. A plump woman sitting directly behind Eleanor spoke.

"That's Richard Bailey. The owner."

For some reason, Eleanor thought of cantankerous George Bailey in her second-favorite movie, *It's a Wonderful Life.*

"He's a doozy." The woman said this with such venom Eleanor was instantly alert, but Audrey was poking her in the ribs.

"Kit, look. Sara just got her horse to back up. It'll be Marylou's turn next."

While their daughters were taught to ride huntseat, to command great splay-footed slunkers named Daisy or Smokey, Mohawk or Lotso Dots, Audrey and Eleanor complained about their lives like pastimes gone wrong, drank bitter coffee, kept to their seats with the other mothers, perched like plain wrens, settling for the hour of lesson, then rising and scattering. When Sara, one blustery March afternoon, wrenched her ankle in the Luthers' unthawed yard, sprawling over one of the little red-and-white horse jumps Neil had made for the girls; when Sara fell as Marylou shot past triumphant on her imaginary steed,

Neil telephoned Audrey while Eleanor ministered to both shrieking girls. The upshot was Sara, on crutches, dropping ou of equitation and Eleanor chauffeuring her daughter in Neil's old, failing Mercedes, Eleanor sitting off by herself, bored witless.

SET ON THE EDGE of one of the county's forest preserves, Country Club Stables was a humid, shoddy warren of dark barns, full of Dickensian passageways. Neil's parents disapproved of these newest lessons, injury being one factor, not to mention the dangerous moral atmosphere brought on by too many foreign grooms. (Neil's mother, Pearl, harped so much on the "low, criminal element" lurking about in stables, somehow equating foreign with criminal, Eleanor began to wonder if there wasn't some failed xenophobic romance in Pearl's life.) But after ice-skating, after ballet (masochism euphemized as "grace"), Eleanor felt intoxicated, hot with pleasure. Horses were erotic, the clichés were true, the snide little jokes. To see men enslaved to horses was sexy enough, but seeing them reduced to grooming and caring for something besides themselves was sexier still. So, during one of the lessons, Eleanor ventured off to explore, which is how she bumped into Mr. Bailey in his standard mustard-colored breeches and tweed jacket the color of spoiled mushrooms. His hair was thick, wavy and silver, his eyes were a plum black, and he looked so disconcertingly like Scarlett's father, Mr. O'Hara, in her third-favorite movie, *Gone*

With the Wind. Eleanor felt herself recoiling and drawing near at the same time. They exchanged a few words, his brusque, hers apologetic; later, she would realize he had sized her up with a sociopath's cold accuracy.

Sitting back in the bleachers, chomping away at a Baby Ruth, was the same heavyset woman, with the unlikely name of Ariel. "Remember the Helen Brach murder case last year?"

Eleanor remembered. She nodded.

"Richard Bailey was dating her when it happened. Remember how they never found the body? A lot of people believe it's buried in these stables, but there's not enough evidence to arrest him. The police are just waiting for him to slip up."

"Heels down, Portia." Ariel half stood up to yell at her daughter, then wheezed down, out of breath and smiling brightly at Eleanor.

"He sells bad racehorses to rich women. But Mrs. Brach was an animal rights activist. My theory is she had the goods on him and was about to blow the whistle."

A murderer! thought Eleanor, alarmed and enchanted.

(Oh Mr., Mr. Johnny Lebec, how could you be so mean?
We told you you'd be sorry for inventing that machine.
Now all the neighbors' cats and dogs will never more be
    seen,

*They've all been ground to sausages in Johnny Lebec's
   machine!)*

If she turned out the light in their upstairs bedroom,
Eleanor could see Neil out in the alley, wearing his old car-
penter's suit, an aluminum work-lamp clamped to the stock-
ade fence, working on Blue Buster. He was repainting it, which
seemed to call for a grinding wheel—her station wagon now
bore huge, leprous patches, scabs, up and down its sides. Over
a month ago, Neil guess-timated it would be a two-week project. Now she saw sparks flying and worried, was he wearing his
Plexiglas goggles? How could he possibly enjoy grinding away at
metal instead of being up here with her? It had become the single mystery of her marriage, the way in which Neil's wild streak
had been rerouted into a seemingly endless list of domestic
projects, most of which narrowly skirted disaster. On her way
down to the kitchen to find some chocolate, Eleanor ticked off
the worst:

—the time Neil decided to stucco rather than rewall-
paper their tiny upstairs bathroom, troweling so much
gunk, like vanilla frosting, onto the chicken-wire frame covering the walls that his father, Bert, who stopped by, told
Eleanor that weight would never hold, and if Neil wasn't
careful—this was no goddamned birthday cake!—the

whole bathroom would kerplunk down into the dining room.

—last Thanksgiving, when Neil polished his grandmother's silverware on the stone grinding wheel in the basement, how his mother, setting the table, said, "What in pete's sake happened to Gigi's silver, this knife's a razor?" and Eleanor was forced to explain how in putting a gleam on his grandmother's silver, Neil had accidentally ground half of it away.

—last summer's Plaster Party, when Neil promised free beer and pizza to all his friends and neighbors who would drop by to help him restucco the bottom half of their house, how the wheelbarrows were churning with fresh-mixed plaster when a guy from Peru named Pato, who somebody had brought along, started screaming because the lime in the mixture was eating away his hands . . . how Eleanor had had to run to the hardware store and charge twenty pairs of Rubbermaid gloves.

—oh, and right after Marylou was born, how Neil insisted on saving money by using cloth diapers and washing them himself . . . then had to wear a gas mask because he'd let them soak in the plastic hamper too long. Neil's projects called for tools that ground things away, for dangerous chemicals, explosives. What would a psychiatrist make of her husband's compulsion to grind to nothing, blow to smithereens, take down the house?

In the kitchen, Eleanor rustled through the pink bag of Brach's milk chocolate peanut clusters. That morning she had stood before the candy shelf at Dominick's, studying three rows of Brach's candies, distributed from a factory in Cicero, Illinois. Wasn't Cicero an old Roman orator, someone who had been assasinated? What if Bailey had disposed of her body at the candy factory, bits of Helen in the vats . . . (*Oh Mr., Mr. Johnny Lebec how could you . . .*)? Eleanor dumped the peanut clusters into the sink, running hot water over them so she could not be tempted to dig through the trash; she knew her own shameless cravings.

Near the back door was the latest stack of Nancy Drew mysteries from the library, long overdue. She carried several upstairs, along with the gray notepad she made lists on. Whenever she had insomnia, lists helped, were soporific. Ordinarily such sleep-inducing lists consisted of chores, obligations, things to remember, variations of short- and long-range goals. These were not dramatic lists, more like lullabies, sleeping potions. But tonight's list kept her unnerved, awake with perverse comparisons:

NANCY DREW
"young, amateur detective"
"attractive, titian-haired detective"
"pretty, titian-haired detective"

CARSON DREW
"the leading attorney in River Heights"
"tall, handsome . . . he and Nancy
    helped each other with cases
    and were close companions"

HANNAH GRUEN
"kindly housekeeper"
"a lovable woman who had lived
    with Nancy and her father
    since the death of Mrs. Drew
    when Nancy was only three"

NED NICKERSON
"Nancy's special friend, a friend of
    long standing, a good-looking
    young man, broad-shouldered
    and deeply tanned, a football
    player . . . they enjoyed the
    same things and frequently
    went together to parties . . .
    though she had many other ad-
    mirers, Nancy admitted that
    Ned was her favorite"

BESS MARVIN
"a pretty, plump blonde, less in-
    clined to adventure than
    George or Nancy"

ELEANOR LUTHER
mother of Marylou
wife of Neil Luther

MORRIS STODDARD
Eleanor's father, a retired ortho-
    dontist who liked to refer to
    Eleanor as a "kook"

OLD MRS. FISK
cranky widow, met in supermarket

NEIL LUTHER
this Christmas, gave Eleanor a fry-
    ing pan and a high-necked flan-
    nel nightgown

ARIEL
large, nosy woman

GEORGE FAYE
"an attractive, tomboyish girl with
   short dark hair"
"a dark, athletic girl, Bess' cousin"
"spunky and proud of having a
   boy's name"

AUDREY
best friend, not related

NANCY'S SPORTY RED COUPE
"given to her by her father, Carson
   Drew, leading attorney, etc."

ELEANOR'S BLUE BUSTER
purchased by Neil from a foul-
   tempered, one-legged man

Instead of sleuthing, didn't she just plod behind Neil and
Marylou, picking up pieces, hardly solving a thing? She was a
bit of domestic equipment, an Osterizer, a toaster, old Gigi's
vacuum, serviceable and sturdy, a clothespin kept going by the
notion she was irreplaceable, special. But was she? Whoever
heard of Nancy Drew's mother? Who cared? She died when
Nancy was three—every girl's wish, father to herself, a harmless
old housekeeper to do the dirty work—oh, mightn't Eleanor's
own life have been a different story?

Perhaps I've stumbled on a clue! Nancy thought excitedly.
from *The Clue Through the Crumbling Wall*
by CAROLYN KEENE

The next morning, as she stood on a chair, hanging cardboard
shamrocks in the bay window of their kitchen alcove, as she
taped cutouts of leaping leprechauns and pots of gold to the
porch windows, Eleanor was forcibly struck by an idea. What if

she changed from frump-o housewife to pert, snappy Nancy Drew, smoking out the evil Mr. Bailey, and solving the murder of the candy heiress? With a leftover leprechaun facedown in her lap, Eleanor sat in the living room, watching the videotape Neil had made to send to her parents in Hawaii—a tour of their newly remodeled kitchen and master bedroom. Eleanor was narrating, somewhat like a First Lady tour of the White House, except that Eleanor appeared stiff and wooden. She looked like a bit of spouse-fruit caught in aspic. That was it. She would trap Mr. Bailey, be his Venus's-flytrap. Hadn't she recently triumphed, proved credible, as eighteen-year-old Madge in *Picnic?*

So when Neil left for a three-day board of directors' meeting in Florida, she rented a titian-colored pageboy wig at the costume shop on Central Street and took to wearing the bustier from *Picnic* under her new, red sweater. Like anyone with a secret existence (her husband for instance), she felt buoyant, revitalized.

> *"Do be careful, my dear. You always start out solving mysteries with the idea you'll be perfectly safe and you always end up getting into hot water."*
>
> Hannah Gruen, in *The Crooked Bannister*
> by CAROLYN KEENE

So easy! To lie! Exhilarating! To take drama off the stage and into one's own life! With Marylou in the arena riding a sway-bellied Appaloosa called Lotso Dots, Eleanor glided, in new, patent leather boots, to the door next to the soda pop machine, the one that said "Richard Bailey, Barn Owner and Manager." She knocked, entered the shoe-box office, swiveling her hips in a Kim Novak kind of way, until Mr. Bailey was on his feet, behind his cluttered desk, offering his villain's hand to her. Eleanor lowered her voice, made it husky.

"Yes, I should like to purchase one of your instruction horses. My name is Eleanor Drew."

He sat down, leaned back, twirled a pencil. "Which one?"

"Lotso Dots."

"Do you have private facilities, Mrs. Drew? Your own facilities?"

"Ms. Drew. I'm a widow. I'm having a barn built along with a new home up in Lake Forest. In the interim, I assume the horse could remain here."

She had never paired deceit with fun! Offstage, which was most of her life, of course, Eleanor had always been excruciatingly earnest. He believed her!

"I'm afraid I cannot sell that particular horse."

"Why ever not?"

"The animal is unsound. It is only used for children's lessons."

Eleanor kept silent. She wished for a cigarette. For a cigarette holder to hold the cigarette.

"I do have other horses for sale."

"Well, my daughter has her heart set. You know how children are. Arbitrary."

"What are you doing tonight, Ms. Drew? Eleanor."

Her tissue of lies thus woven, Eleanor exited, having accepted a dinner date with the suspected slayer of Helen Brach. Marylou could sleep over at Audrey's, though Eleanor would have to lie about her own whereabouts. Fib to Neil, too, when he called, as he did at eleven o'clock, as if punctuality equaled fidelity. Hah.

But Sara had been dropped off at her grandparents' in Palatine, so that Audrey could sleep with her estranged husband, Sara's father. This was a complicated story Eleanor had heard about numerous times but could never keep straight. Sometimes she pictured herself raising the roofs off all the houses up and down her desperately tidy block, peering down like a giantess at all the square little scenes of pandemonium, room after room of high-pitched squalor. Eleanor wound up calling old Mrs. Fisk, the balding, shadow version of capable, kindly Hannah Gruen. When she was a girl, Eleanor had longed for a housekeeper to replace her mother. She longed for one now. It seemed the penultimate luxury, although the one time Neil had treated her to a cleaning woman, Eleanor found herself tidying up before the woman arrived, then tagging behind her, then fixing them both a substantial lunch so she could hear more of this woman's life story, which, if true, was unbelievable, then having to clean the house a second time before Neil got home to complain he'd been robbed.

Yes, old Mrs. Fisk was available. So Eleanor rented *National*

Velvet and *Brigadoon,* and with a slick frosting of Nair on her upper lip, fixed Marylou's favorite supper, pigs in blankets. She began to see how guilt disguised itself as solicitude. There she was, a married woman, a mother, impersonating a wealthy widow, meeting a murderer for cocktails. Reasons for this had become ephemeral, slippery as eels. Because she wanted to crime-solve? Punish Neil? Have an adventure? No. She shouldn't do this. This was going too far.

Too late. Mrs. Fisk was on the couch, knitting a hideous orange-and-brown-checkered afghan while Marylou pranced a platoon of My Little Ponies, Sea Splash, Moonshadow, Princess and Glory, up, down and between her sitter's trousered legs.

"Here's the number where I'll be, Mrs. Fisk. Marylou's bedtime is eight o'clock, and she has permission to sleep in her My Little Pony tent tonight."

Mrs. Fisk sat there, Sea Splash perched on top of her wispy, waspy head. There was something amiss with the woman; what a last resort she was. Eleanor had long ago dropped out of the neighborhood baby-sitting coop. Too depressing, poking about other people's homes, snooping, which is what she always succumbed to, raw snooping.

She arrived at Hackney's, what Audrey called a hangout for the horsey set. She stood in the small dark lobby until her eyes adjusted, until she saw Mr. Bailey waving her over—he had his own table! He stood up, shook her hand, and she took note of his gold eyetooth. Out of his barn, he looked like the criminal he was, flashy, avaricious, sly. She had thought to pull a bag of Brach's buttermints out of her purse, nudge them onto the table, but immediately realized how childish a notion that had been. It was as if some part of her were still Marylou's age, still acting out.

Throughout dinner, Eleanor confabulated. Proved mendacious, chock a block with fibbery. Lying through her teeth made her delirious. And Mr. Bailey was clearly flirting with her. Eleanor excused herself to go to the ladies' room. She swayed past other couples, huddled intimately in wooden booths. Perhaps this was a den of thieves and murderers, no-souls, a Dantean lower rung. Who knew? In the bathroom, she zeroed her face close to the spotty mirror. Oopsie. Some of her navy eyeliner had smeared under one eye. Her wig needed readjusting, a lick of her own red hair was poking through. On the way back, she determined to ask Mr. Bailey—Richard—all about himself. Draw him out. So far she had talked on and on, answering all his questions about her made-up self. What would spring his lock? Should she ask about his father? His childhood? What would Drew have done? For one, she would never have downed three martinis.

But he was gone. Nope, she found him up front, paying the bill and sucking, detestably, on a toothpick.

"I'd like to show you the horses I have for sale. You should ride, you know, not just your daughter."

"I don't know how."

"I could teach you. Private lessons, Eleanor. You have excellent posture."

She followed his shiny black Mercedes in Neil's white, ailing one, careful to keep the spiked tip of her high heel from catching in the floorboard, praying the car would chug stolidly along. He walked her through a series of barns; it grew noticeably darker, more isolated, more stalls were empty. For a moment, Eleanor entertained the scenario that this man was going to topple her into a bed of straw, demand she write him a fat check, slay then bury her in the horse-smelling dirt, smack beside Mrs. Brach. Eleanor lagged, observed how bandy-legged he was, how he walked with an unpleasant, cocky swagger. It had not escaped her detective's attention that his employees treated him with a mix of servility, fear and something slightly mutinous, ripe for betrayal. He had no friends among his help, she had seen that. Probably no friends at all. Now, in what must be the darkest, farthest barn of all, he waited for her, then very lightly, began to steer her this way and that as they moved. When she stumbled, he caught her at the waist, and she thought she smelled aftershave coming from underneath his maroon turtleneck. Turtle neck? She had an insane impulse to giggle. Hardy-har. Instead, she hiccuped.

"Here he is. Thoroughbred. Four years old."

"An ex-racehorse?" Hiccuped again.

"Very good. How did you know? I've got this other one for sale as well. Over here."

He did not love these horses; she could see that. They were investments, horseflesh. Such a contrast to Marylou. He was hypnotizing her. She felt drugged. Had Mrs. Brach stood here like this? Were these the same horses he had tried to sell her? She felt Mrs. Brach hovering nearby. Her corpse might be lodged somewhere under Eleanor's unsteady feet, but her busybody ghost was darting about.

"Horses are among the most sensual creatures on earth. I have learned a great deal just being near them." Saying this, he tightened his arm around Eleanor's waist, drew her close, an odd sensation as he was a good two feet shorter, a pip-squeak really, but what a tribute to his criminal seductiveness that she allowed him, that she could imagine him leading her into an empty stall, nudging her dress up over her hips, over her head (after which he would be confronted with the bustier, with having to wrestle it off her). But then Eleanor's purse slipped off her shoulder, hitting the dirt with a soft ploffing sound. The bag of Brach's buttermints tumbled out.

He was smooth as silk, pushing the pink-and-purple-striped bag back into her purse, slipping its strap back up her arm. One of the horses stretched out its long neck, to stare at her.

"I have to go."

"Oh no. It's much too early. Let's just go for a little drive. I want to show you something."

SO ELEANOR SAT, hiccuping in Mr. Bailey's car, which smelled of tobacco and something else (*fee fi fo fum* . . . blood? bone?), sailing right past Mrs. Brach's mansion (which Eleanor had seen before), a bloated old colonial, with an ostentatious, brass-tipped iron fence in front of its circular drive, like an embassy gate, and fat lot of good it had done in saving the poor woman. Was Eleanor imagining that Richard Bailey took his foot off the gas, the car slowing to a snail's pace, as they passed the house? He was drinking from a flask now, offering her a swig, but she had to keep her wits about her, so Eleanor refused. Just past the Brach mansion, he swung the car down a steep narrow road that led to a small parking lot hemmed in by large, dark trees. The parking lot was empty, and beyond it, she knew, for she had taken Marylou to this beach several times last summer, was the lake. When he came around to her side, opened the door and held out his hand, Eleanor took note of his black leather gloves. Where had those come from? Gripping her hand with alarming strength, he walked Eleanor down a small set of tiered wooden steps. There was the playground, the curly slide, merry-go-round, bucket swings, unmoving and ghostly, ominous without children or the sounds of children. They scuffed through the sand to the edge of the lake, where a silvery jumble of alewives, lake fish small as clothespins, had washed up dead. Eleanor felt gloomy. Philosophical. He still had not spoken and now stood, gloved hands clasped behind his back, facing a lake vast and treacherous enough to suggest the sea. People lost their lives to its waters every year. She was convinced he was not thinking of the lake, but of what was directly above him, on the land above him, the silent, unlit accusation of Helen Brach's mansion. What if he had actually cared for her? What if Helen had been an unpleasant, uncouth or even a hateful person? Being murdered put one so completely out of reach. She glanced at Richard Bailey, saw the tragic almost noble cast of his profile. Then he spat into the water, turned abruptly and without a glance at her or a word of explanation, started back to the car, not even gazing up toward the mansion he had no doubt slept in and dreamed of owning one day.

Eleanor traipsed behind him, thinking that both the wild success and flaw of all Nancy Drew mysteries was this: Nancy was absurdly straightforward—no neuroses, no contradictions to muddle the plot's formulaic thrust. The dangerous fact was, Eleanor found Mr. Bailey, gold-toothed, short and villainous, surprisingly attractive.

On the drive back to Morton Grove, neither said a thing. Eleanor was still trying to decide where the evening was headed when Mr. Bailey parked his car in the spot that said Manager, got out, opened her door and formally walked her to Neil's white Mercedes. After she had gotten in, she cranked down the window.

"Thank you so much, Richard. I'll think about those horses."

"Oh, I've no doubt you will. Kit. Mooser. Eleanor Luther." His black-gloved hands gripped the window, his fingers murderously flexing, unflexing.

"You ridiculous fool. What game are you running on me?"

He reached in to take hold of what? Her neck? Eleanor stamped her foot on the accelerator and shot past. She glanced in the rearview mirror, but saw nothing. Had she run over his foot? His feet? Oh mustard. Fine. Once home, Eleanor, sprung from her own trap, found Mrs. Fisk snoring on her afghan, Marylou asleep in her Pony tent, and Neil phoning for the third time.

Dave exclaimed, "What a narrow escape!"

from *The Message in the Hollow Oak*
by CAROLYN KEENE

The last riding lesson involved a competition with colored ribbons, pale pink, green, red, blue. Neil videotaped Marylou while Eleanor sat thinking how she did not like the secrecy of a secret life. It was, after all, no fun. She was camouflaged in case Richard Bailey was around, wearing a floppy camping hat, huge sunglasses (what Marylou called her "fly eyes") and one of Neil's baggy sweatsuits, the color of potato skins. Portia's mother, Ariel, whose detective skills were clearly superior to Eleanor's, recognized her instantly. When Neil crossed the arena to get a better shot, Ariel leaned conspiratorially forward.

"Did you hear the latest? Someone took a can of red spray paint to the pavement outside the Brach house. RICHARD BAILEY . . . YOU'RE IT . . . THE MURDERER! Everyone hates that man. I'm going to drive past this afternoon to see it again." She raised her book, a paperback with a black cover and lurid red splashes. "True crime. I'm addicted to the stuff."

It was then that Eleanor had the strangest sense that her discontent was not peculiar, not even original. There were hosts of women eager to spy on Richard Bailey, to go down his villainous path. Ingenues like her, artless and aging, finding out too late that goodness was not its own reward, was no reward at all. Children left home, husbands betrayed. Go on, Eleanor, do it. Go on. Raise the roofs off the tidy dwellings up and down your block, blow the roofs off all the houses everywhere, take courage and peer in, breathe in scandal, the murderous secret, the putrid whiff of sin. But aren't there just as many rooms, like schoolroom dioramas, where wives sit heavy and still, bewildered sleuths, their beds all unmade, clues fine as dust, asking "what now, what now?"

Later that night, when she looked to Neil, about to ask, when he fell into it like her straight man, asking *What, Kit? What is it?* Eleanor Luther did what she could, what was left in her character to do—she looked away.

What are you going to do now, Nancy, without a mystery to solve?" Bess teased.

Her friend smiled. "Work on the sweater I'm knitting for Ned." She did not know then that she soon would become involved in The Secret of the Red Gate Farm.

But George knew that Nancy and mystery were never far apart. She gave a sigh of mock sadness.

"Poor Ned! I hope he doesn't need that sweater very soon!"

from *The Secret of Shadow Ranch* by CAROLYN KEENE

High Fidelity

$\mathcal{L}$ouden, Prell Luther's fiancé, and his oldest friend, Dirk, have him—their Peeping Tom—trussed up in a Turkish carpet. Louden squats at one end, digging oily fingers into a can of sardines. Dirk lounges at the other with what looks to be a Maglite sliding off his narrow brick of belly. In her pink gingham baby dolls, Prell does a complicated fairy leap over the rolled up rug.

Dirk raises his neck, swivels his head to spit into his plastic chew cup. "Perverted enchilada."

"No more peeps out of you," Prell fwumps down in the middle. "I should poke your two bad eyes out. Blind pig in a blanket."

"What the hell?" Prell's little sister, Suave, has just stumbled out of her fetid, blighted room where she's been sleeping on the floor with Cara and Bree, six rough knees and six grimy elbows hooked into a Chinese puzzle ring. Squinting outside, Suave sees the plastic snowman, still plugged in, glowing weakly, though the Arizona sun is blinding. Beyond that, under a shaggy queen palm, parked like a shipwreck, is Louden's lime-green muscle car. "Sheez. It's hot as blazes."

Louden's mouth is oily and full. "We caught the creep. Took all friggin' night but we nabbed him. Dirk was set to shoot and claim self-defense."

"Damn straight. A pervert's about as useful as a screen door on a submarine."

"So who'd they catch, Prell?" Suave moves nearer the wine-colored roll, fatter at one end. What if it's someone they know? A neighbor—the fire chief in his skimpy red shorts, or the retired ophthalmologist crouched like a plaster dwarf in his rosebed, or the orange-whiskered Scottish bachelor who's writing a thriller based on the true confessions of convicted sex offenders. Or, God forbid, it's Mr. Rungren, who last Sunday carried over one of his wife's peanut butter pies just to say he'd been raised the old-fashioned way, to call women ladies, but an exception had to be made for three firecracker redheads under one incendiary roof. God, what if it was old Mr. Rungren at her feet?

"He won't tell us his name. He seems kind of what, what would you say, Dirk?"

"Oh, like the lights are all blazing but nobody's home." Dirk is clipping his toenails—click, click, click. "Suave. Prell. Aren't those shampoos? How come you guys call yourselves shampoo names?"

Louden shoots his hand up in the air. "Answer! These two have a pact never to let a man they don't approve of into their house. It's a female stronghold. Impregnable. Except for me. I've impregnated it."

"What's that got to do with shampoo?"

"Suave and I had this act when we were kids. We wrapped

towel turbans on our heads and sailed our Ken dolls out the windows, singing 'I'm Gonna Wash That Man Right Out of My Hair.' You heard that song?"

"Nope," yawned Dirk.

"Prell, can I see him? Maybe it's one of the Christian kids from school who hate me."

"Looking in my window? Hoping to see me naked? I don't think so. I'd suggest the end nearest the TV."

On her hands and knees, Suave peers in. "Jeepers. Can he unroll?"

Louden is licking sardine oil off each of his fingers. "Little chump's trussed up tighter than a Christmas ham."

"Little?" Suave sees the dark, curly top of a small head.

"Suave, come over here." Prell whispers in her ear. "They caught some fat, nerdy kid and they've decided to spook him, then let him go. Teach him a lesson."

"Scare him?"

"Yup. Scare the peewadden out of him."

"Oh. When's Mah get home?" Their mother, Nora, had gone to a Romance Writers of America Convention in Long Beach. As Pearl Marvel, her nom de plume, she had been one of the featured speakers, her topic, "The Virtues of Faithfulness," which neither Prell nor Suave could understand, since she had been cheated on in both of her marriages. "Maybe that's the point," Suave had suggested.

"Sometime tonight I think."

"Prell, my sexy saucer of milk. I leave for work in eighteen minutes." Louden has a job as a telemarketer, selling home first-aid kits. He's saving for the wedding Prell hasn't yet told him won't be happening, not in a million years. "Will you keep the ladies company, Dirk?"

"You bet. I'm thinking of getting a job as a whadyacallit, one of those guys that serves orders of protection. I like the idea of defending defenseless women."

Prell and Suave nudge one another.

"Actually, I think I'll take this little rug chump for a long, special ride, how 'bout it, Louden. Right? Let's go."

Dirk and Louden each hoist an end onto one shoulder, march the struggling carpet out the door.

PRELL AND DIRK are on the sofa, watching Homer Simpson. Prell's got her bare legs stretched across Dirk's lap.

"Holy cats. Forest legs."

"Suave's worse. She stopped shaving weeks ago."

"Blech. Why?"

"She says as long as women's grooming habits are shaped by men's desires, we're still in a patriarchy."

"A what?"

"A man's world. We're still in a man's world. Suave and her friends are reviving the lost matriarchy. I think our house is first. A sort of trial balloon."

"Oh."

"Dirk, honey, would you rub my feet a little? I swear, besides Louden, you are just the sweetest man. Wherever did you take that nasty child?"

"We dropped him in front of his house, rolled up on the front lawn."

"How did you find out where he lived?"

"We asked."

SUAVE IS IN HER TENT, eavesdropping. For the last five years, she's had a one-man tent pitched in the living room, loaded with books . . . she'll crawl in for hours, sometimes a whole day, only to emerge for food. Nora and Prell are in awe of her, think she's a possible genius, when half the time Suave's just hiding out. Prell's reading consists of *Cosmo* articles on how to hold the male gaze ten seconds, look away, brush ever so lightly against him. Right now she wants to marry a Bugsy Siegel Mafia-type and be a lounge singer in a platinum-blond wig. Last month she had been fourth runner-up in the Miss Gilbert pageant. (*Suave, you should have seen, every last one of those girls taped her pubic hair with duct tape under her bathing suit . . . you should have seen their faces when they saw mine was not only untaped but dyed purple.*) Suave and Nora, in the third row of chairs inside the junior high cafeteria, had been thrilled to see Prell onstage in a top hat and tails, twirling a cane, singing "Chicago,

Chicago," though she'd started out in a most baffling way, dedicating her performance to "a very special person who believed in her more than anyone in the world." As Nora waited expectantly, half out of her chair, Prell said a name Nora'd never even heard of, a great-aunt Delrina. After the pageant, wolfing down two triple cheeseburgers, Prell confessed to inventing Delrina. "God, never again, no more pageants for me . . . It's all starve and smile, starve and smile."

For years now, Suave had watched men drop like Pet Rocks around her sister, not because she had long, crimpy red hair (Suave had that, so did her mother), not because she had an ivoried, pretty face (Suave did too, so did her mother). It was some other, floaty quality, giddy and conscienceless. Prell denied herself nothing, emitted guiltless, carnal radiance. The fact was, even though her sister was her favorite person in the world, Suave recognized that Prell cared about people, mainly men, for the attention they could provide her. Suave imagined herself smoking with Prell's dramatic abandon, eating hamburgers with a blank conscience, in contrast to her own sparse, broody vegan diet. (She even wore black Mary Jane–style vegetable shoes, ordered from London.) Suave felt a profound aversion to humanity, she felt obligated to defend hopeless causes. This had made her a social outcast while her sister bobbled about with impunity, a jolly pink balloon. If Suave tried constantly to mend the world's moral fractures, Prell was rarely around to see the bitter trail of heartbreak she left behind. The last thing Suave could remember Prell shedding tears over was the death of Princess Diana. Prell had knotted an enormous black silk scarf around her head, and carried a single white rose to a memorial service held in the pouring rain in a park somewhere. She came home around midnight, drenched, saying there had only been twenty people there, all elderly women, but it had been unutterably beautiful. She had made up her mind, during her mourning, to move to London and marry Prince William.

Worst had been last year, the day after Christmas, when Prell disappeared. She had worked with Nora and Suave on Christmas Day at a local Salvation Army kitchen. Wearing a short, tight red dress, Prell handed out cheap, unwrapped toys and flirted with all the homeless men while her mother spooned gravy onto hundreds of breast-sized hills of mashed potatoes. For weeks before her disappearance, Prell had been calling herself Sidney Robinson, hanging out near the university, sitting on sidewalks making hemp jewelry with other Rainbow People (a sort of migratory New Age tribe, Suave explained to her mother). For two days, Nora was sleepless and frantic, circling and recircling the phone, until an ambulance service somewhere in Alabama called, asking for Sidney Robinson's mother. That was it, Prell was dead. Nora nearly lost consciousness waiting for the poor connection to clear, but it was a man named Charles who told her he had spotted two girls by the side of a country road, hitchhiking, and being the father of four girls himself, he'd brought them back to the ambulance station, cooked them a square meal, then volunteered to drive them all the way to Key West himself. He wanted Nora to know her daughter was just fine, and put Prell on the phone to say "Hi, Mommy," just like a contrite two-year-old.

Two weeks later, Prell called again. Her friend Heather had split, Prell had last eaten three days before, she thought, at a soup kitchen. Everyone in the trailer where she was staying (how many people can cram together in a trailer, thought Nora, it sounds like eggs in a carton), had some kind of pneumonia thing, and she was sick, too. So Nora wired money and three days later, at midnight, picked up her runaway child at the Greyhound station in downtown Phoenix. It was January, and Prell wavered on the curb in a thin cotton shift and a little religious-looking cap, her unwashed and dreadlocked hair stuffed underneath. Her voice was ethereal, lacey with fever, and when Nora gathered her daughter up in her arms, all she felt was scouring heat and bones. Prell weighed less than ninety pounds. After she got better, stronger, Prell cleaned houses in the neighborhood by day and impersonated Marilyn Monroe by night, while watching Louden play pool. What money she earned, Prell invested in animal rescue. She had a ball python (along with baggies of frozen white mice, mousicles, Nora called them), Stevie Ray, a blind, brindle-coated puppy with fluorescent teeth, and a three-legged box turtle that trundled out from under the sofa to eat a banana, then disappeared for months at a time. Prell's latest job was cooking two vegetarian meals per day for a cult of ten adults wearing white dust masks. They had interviewed Prell in their living room, standing in a circle around her, videotaping her as she sat on a plain wooden chair and swore an oath she neither smoked nor consumed meat of any kind.

"Thanks Dirk," Prell waggled her newly massaged toes. "Those people are the creepiest. They wear little muzzle masks that deaden their voices, and they only unhook them to eat. Then there's this miniscule dying poodle they keep pumping full of oxygen. I've run out of recipe ideas. All I can think of is grilled cheese. I can't believe these people live only three blocks away in this very ordinary-looking house. Suave says only 26 percent of Americans live in a traditional nuclear family any-more. The rest of us are in cults and God knows what-all. I'm quitting. What if they are homicidal? I quit. Tell Louden if I don't come home tomorrow, to check their basement."

SUAVE'S STACKING LIBRARY BOOKS and magazine articles all over the dining room table. *Sixty-seven Ways to Save the An-imals, Old MacDonald's Factory Farm, So You Want to Become an Activist?, Poisoned Chicken, Poisoned Egg.* She's snipping pic-tures from magazines and stick-gluing them onto a giant piece of green posterboard, then attaching quotes written on index cards:

"Animals bred or captured for dissection suffer the traumas

of confinement, transport, callous handling, often inadequate food and inhumane killing methods."

"Frogs' spinal cords frequently are not properly severed (pithed) before dissection. When this happens, frogs are dissected while still conscious."

"Every year, 5.7 million frogs, rats, mice, rabbits, chipmunks, sharks, pigs, cats and dogs are dissected by junior and senior high school students."

Suave's rehearsing her grisly quotes, muttering them aloud, when Dirk passes by, headed for the kitchen.

"What's with all the books, Suave? Yeesh. What the heck is this? He shakes the cereal bowl. Paste? Why is there a spoon in it?"

"It's tofu. I refuse to dissect frogs and fetal pigs in biology so the teacher's making me do a presentation instead." Suave doesn't add that yesterday, someone snuck up behind her in hall and dropped icy frog guts down her neck. Every day she deals with hate and homophobic prejudice on a scale she cannot get her mother or even her sister to believe.

"What's this stuff made of anyway? This toefoo stuff?"

"Soybeans."

"Hey. What's this? A bunny-go-round?"

The picture in the book Dirk's pointing to shows white rabbits locked into heavy iron collars in a laboratory wheel.

Suave sighs. "Those are laboratory rabbits being subjected

to Baize testing, that's where their eyelids are held back with metal clips so they can't blink and various chemicals are dropped into their eyes and left there for days to determine the effects. Most of them break their necks or backs struggling to escape from the pain. After the tests they're killed."

"Why do they do that?"

"So women can wear blue eye shadow without getting an allergic reaction."

"You're depressing, Suave. Has anyone ever told you that? How come you pay attention to stuff like that?"

She looks at him. "Because if I don't, who will?"

SUAVE WENT WITH Bree and Cara to school. She carried her green posterboard off to war, into the fray, into another day of being shunned, of her queer-vegan-atheist soul being publically prayed over at lunchtime by the New Fundamentalists. Suave is giving serious thought to organizing an antiprayer vigil where she and her friends would take turns reciting from Bertrand Russell's *Why I Am Not a Christian*.

At three, Prell speeds up to the school's entrance in Dirk's red Cadillac convertible, blasting Patsy Cline's "I Fall to Pieces." With her rhinestone-studded, winged sunglasses and turquoise chiffon scarf, she looks like a fifties Hollywood star. Like Rita Hayworth. "Hi, boys!" She offers a parade wave to a group of football jocks who hate Suave and her queer-vegan-atheist friends. Last week, they'd "accidentally" slammed one of Jason's hands in a locker, so he couldn't play the harp at the school concert.

"Stop it, Prell. Cut it out. Those guys hate me. Where's Dirk?" Stevie Ray, the blind puppy with ghoulish teeth, is wombling around on the front seat.

"Oh, a friend picked him up. He had some job thingy. How was school?"

"Terrible. The whole class started flipping frog hearts, lungs and livers around the room. Mr. Nord spent the rest of the class ranting about respect for life. How hypocritical is that?"

They stop at Thrift Outlet, and Prell, who has a weakness for fusty glamour, buys three old prom dresses and a polka-dot negligee, while Suave, who collects men's bowling and gas station shirts, finds a pair of powder blue Sansabelt slacks and white buck golf shoes with cleats. As they turn the corner near their house, they see a yellow taxi out front.

"Mah!"

"Yeah, but who's with her?" A tall, well-built man with a long, silky dark brown ponytail is lifting a suitcase out of the trunk.

Prell goes into her TV-commercial voice. *"I can't believe it's not butter!"*

"Where'd Mah go? I can't even see her."

"Somewhere to the left of Fabio. She's our original shrimpette."

"Which reminds me, Prell. No shrimp. Don't eat shrimp.

Shrimp-trawling nets are endangering the sea turtles, especially the Kemp's Ridley and the loggerheads."

"Fuck's sake, Suave. What's left to eat in your world?"

They're watching Fabio hold their mother's hand, standing beside the plastic snowman left over from Christmas, laughing at something she's just said.

"Oh bother." Prell scoops up Stevie Ray. "Last time it was that black weight-trainer who dressed like a spandex pirate and was a mere fifteen years younger than Mah."

"Prell, that was over a year ago. How come you get to have men swarming all over you, and Mah can't have a single boyfriend?"

"Suave. Is your memory that parched? I'm protecting you, at least until you're out of high school. Mah's adorable, we love her, but face it, her man radar is way off, shot to pieces. Let's just play this by ear."

"What if he's an exception?"

"There are no exceptions, Suave. None."

Suave trails her sister into the house, remembering how her dad was when she visited him last summer in Albuquerque, how Neil's main occupation seemed to be smoking pot while taking poor aim with his Civil War pistol at field mice skittering through his run-down adobe house.

FABIO TURNS OUT to be a Bolivian movie star living in Santa Monica, eking out a living as a model, actor, substitute teacher.

He'd mostly gotten parts as Native American warriors, shamans, medicine men or an honest sheriff named Whitehorse in an evil desert town. "I died a lot last year," he says with charming modesty. Suave has never seen anyone so handsome in her life, and here he is, sitting on one of their kitchen chairs, watching every move Mah makes. Suave's mother is pouring iced tea into glasses and chirping.

"Oh hi, girls. I'd like you to meet Eduardo. Eduardo, this is my youngest, Maryanne. My oldest, Marylou, is around somewhere. Eduardo and I met at the conference, he was this year's model for the Native American romance series. He's part Incan, Spanish and German. Isn't that the most thrilling combination? Anyway, he's asked me to drive him to Tucson tomorrow, where he starts shooting a movie-of-the-week."

"You're an actor?" Prell materialized in the doorway, clutching a pastel froth of outdated prom dresses. She still had her rhinestone sunglasses on, and her dark red lipstick is slightly smudged. Jeez, thinks Suave. Prell's ruthless when stalking prey. Stevie Ray pretzels around Prell's ankles before rolling with a pitiable yelp, into the wall.

"Well, yes," he laughs, leaning down to tease the puppy with his long, elegant fingers. "When I can get work. It's frankly not much of a part. I play a Comanche war chief who gets shot off his horse by a disgruntled cavalry officer and dragged away in the mud. I don't even have lines. Still, it pays the bills."

"Wow," breathes Prell. "That is so incredibly awesome. Oh, that's Stevie Ray. He's blind."

"WOULD YOU ALL LIKE something to eat?" Here it comes, Mah's famous man-chirp. Over Eduardo's sleek, handsome head, Prell and Suave connect gazes. Mah never believed it, so Prell swore one day she'd tape record her talking whenever a man was around (which has become less and less often), and play it back to her. "Would you like something tweet?" That's how it sounded. *Tweet.* Around men, sudden and unusual accents leaked into Mah's speech, Irish, Hispanic, Texan, or sometimes she sounded like some crotchety British spinster in a baggy cardigan. "I don't know," Mah would sigh, "maybe I should have been a stage actress. I'd get out more."

"Are you staying for dinner?" Prell lowers her sunglasses, leveling her most bewitching gaze on Eduardo, who is watching Mah bend over in front of the refrigerator. Her voice filters out, crisp. "Actually, I've invited Eduardo to spend the night." Mah sometimes complained it was no easy thing, living with two beautiful daughters in the same house. "It can take the wind right out of my sails," she'd say.

SUAVE FOLLOWS PRELL into her room where she is cha-chaing into a pair of black stretch capris and a leopard-print top. "Where are my black mules," she says, rummaging around on the floor of her closet. "Oh well," she pulls out a pair of red spiked heels.

"Spike heels increase the degree to which a woman's butt sticks out by over 4 percent. I read that somewhere."

"You read too much. Anyway, that's the point. Here, precious," Prell coos, lifting the python out of its glass tank with the fake jungle background, letting it wind in an *S* up her arm and drape like a *U* around her neck. "Well, what do you think of him?"

Suave likes Eduardo. She sees him as courtly and literate, a character out of a Jane Austen novel or a prince in a fairy tale, come to their quaint home in the suburbs to save them, or their mother at least. But from what? Who knew? But she didn't want Prell messing it up, flirting with him. Suave knew her sister's treacherous need for male attention. "I think he likes Mah."

"You think?" Prell is lining her top eyelids with liquid liner. Suave is about to say something about cosmetic testing on animals but just then Mah taps on Prell's door and slips in, her face rosy as a girl's. She looks younger than Prell, maybe younger than Suave who is beginning to think age, as a benchmark of anything, is deceptive.

The python jerks, contracts into a *W*, hisses.

"Mah! You'll stop his heart."

"Sorry. You going out with Louden, Marylou? That certainly is an exotic outfit." She sounds dubious, meaning she hates it.

"Maryanne, sweetie, do me a flavor? I need to change out of these airplane clothes. Would you mind keeping Eduardo company? Isn't he nice, girls? Too good to be true? I should pinch myself."

"Mah," Prell says dryly. "No need to pinch. He's real. And Suave's sure he likes you."

"You think? How can you tell? How does one tell these things? I'm so nervous. I'm a wreck. You'd think a romance writer would be able to tell these things. How can you tell?"

Suave shrugs. "Just a feeling."

"But you'll visit with him while I change?"

"Sure she will," says Prell. "We both will. I'll start dinner and Suave can tell him how everything I'm cooking is polluted, poisoned and brought to our kitchen by politically corrupt means. It'll be fun."

Nora hesitates in the doorway, nonplussed by her daughter's tone. Of the three of them, she is somehow the most naive. Suspended in a clear aspic of innocence.

Suave is worried what Mah will change into. Whenever she's insecure, her mother reverts to long bunchy skirts, big peasant blouses and noisy earrings, a style Prell calls Just So You Know I Was a Hippie in 1970 . . .

"Prell, give Mah a chance."

Just then they hear someone playing the piano, not playing, really, more of a jab-plink, jab-plink, an I'll nail "Unchained Melody" if it kills me.

"Prell, I'm serious. I think he's the Exception."

Prell is gluing on false eyelashes, one lash at a time. Suave has a headache from all the fumes in the room. Lately she worries she is oversensitizing herself. Everything makes her sick.

"A test at least," says Prell. "A random test or two."

"Like the tests in a fairy tale?"

"Exactly. The prince, in this case Eduardo, has to pass certain tests before he can have his princess, that would be Mah, old royal in the woods waiting to be plucked from her lowly plight or whatever, but first he must pass his tests. Then they can fall in love, dadidah, all that, be King and Queen, which probably isn't as fun as it looks in books."

The piano stops plinking.

"Here's a test, Suavie. How 'bout I mention the night Mom jumped on the hood of Louden's car in her flannel pajamas, slid off and then broke off his car door."

"No. That makes her sound crazy."

"She was crazy. OK. How 'bout I ever-so-casually mention her ex-husbands?"

"Prell, I don't think so. Let's just do our Stuckey's routine. Something that doesn't make Mah look weird."

"Something that makes us look weird instead?"

"Yeah. Exactly."

WHEN SHE GETS to the living room, Eduardo is on the sofa, paging through one of Suave's library books.

"Want to see my class project? It's in Mom's office, where she writes her books."

"Green or red?" Prell fills the doorway like an exotic jungle bloom. "Spaghetti, I mean."

Eduardo looks at her, notes the python, doesn't bat an eye. "Whichever you'd prefer," he smiles dazzlingly, a Pearl Drops ad, then follows Suave into Mah's office while telling her about the handkerchief-sized moths and butterflies in Bolivia, cockroaches big as house cats. How kids attach string leashes, give them pet names.

He sits cross-legged on the floor, studies her posterboard with meticulous attention, asks her opinion, supports her moral outrage. He mentions his business background in third-world development, his frequent trips home to Bolivia, his dream to return there permanently, find a way to educate through art. Suave is enraptured. Meanwhile, Prell stands in the kitchen over a steaming kettle of pasta, the python like a thick brown whip slung around her neck, the cordless phone to her ear, canceling her date with Louden and quitting her job with the masked cultists.

"SO WHAT'S BEEN your biggest part," Prell asks, twirling and untwirling her spaghetti.

"A Spanish priest in a movie I filmed last summer in Buenos Aires. Father Humberto. He was paraplegic and in love with the village prostitute who, it turns out, was his lost half-sister."

"Good lord. What was your smallest part," asks Mah, eager to keep up. Pete's sake, thinks Suave, now do I get to ask what was your most medium part?

Prell is shrieking. "No! that's my all-time favorite movie! Suave, did you hear that? Eduardo played Keanu Reeves's eyes in *Dracula*."

Eduardo explains how the film had been shot and finished, Keanu Reeves was on location somewhere, when the director realized he needed a close-up shot of Keanu's eyes in one important scene. "So there was this audition, and my eyes got the part."

"That is so cool," says Prell. "We'll rent the movie just to find your eyes."

Suave is beginning to feel sorry for Eduardo. The more he talked, the more his actor's life seemed demeaning. Auditioning to be someone else's eyes, he was worth so much more than that! Next he'd be saying he'd been Brad Pitt's ear or a potted palm behind Johnny Depp. That's probably how most actors' lives were. Scraping by on parts, parts of parts, auditioning for the body parts of stars. She couldn't bear to think of it.

"Anybody ever heard of goggle therapy?" Suave begins telling them about a Harvard psychiatrist who discovered that by covering up one or the other of his patient's eyes, they experienced dramatic shifts in mood, how looking out of one eye encouraged an optimistic side of the brain, while looking out the other produced, literally, a pessimistic, gloomy view.

"Let's play," says Prell, clapping a hand over her right eye. They all sit at the dining room table, cupping first one eye, then the other, reporting various sensations and moods.

"My right eye is manic," says Prell. "The left's depressive."

Mah has her right eye covered, saying it makes her feel introspective and dreamy. "My writing eye," she declares. Suave notices Eduardo regarding her mother with intense interest. Suddenly, he ting-tings on his water glass with the tip of a knife.

"Nora, tell us all about your famous books. Too much time has been spent talking about my depressing life as a scarcely employed actor. Tell us about your latest book. Your newest romance."

Using spoons, napkins, crusts of garlic bread, votive candles and blushing prettily, Nora outlines the triple-intersecting plot of *High Fidelity,* her latest book, which she admits hasn't sold well, her agent saying a triple plot touting the virtue of fidelity was too complicated, too dull, her fans craved infidelities. Blatant cheatings.

Prell does nothing to hide her impatience. Though she hasn't, she acts as if she has heard this umpteen times. "Hey, Mah, speaking of triple plots, which of your two or was it three husbands was the model for the serial killer in *Lost in Mayan Temples?*"

"You have had two or possibly three husbands?" Eduardo looks amused and if possible, more fascinated with Mah. Again, Suave admires his gleaming teeth.

"I'm afraid so. Two marriages does seem to suggest a low fidelity on someone's part. The truth is, Eduardo, I never dated, I was pathologically shy, so I jumped straight into each marriage. Two, very nearly three of them. Does that sound, if not less foolish, at least less sinister? In Italian the word *sinistre* means 'left.'"

Exasperated, Prell has gotten up to plug in the red chili pepper lights along the back patio. She puts on a Louis Armstrong CD. Then she and Suave head into the kitchen to wash dishes and fix dessert.

"You know what, Suave? I like Dirk. Or did until . . ."

"No. You like the man's Cadillac."

"He's big and dumb and sweet. You know what he told me? He wants to adopt Stevie Ray. He's even offered to pay for his eye surgery."

"Gee, that's nice of him. Hey, come here. Quick."

Prell goes and stands by her sister. They both look through the dining room into the living room.

"You ever seen Mah dance, Prell?"

"Once, when she was drunk at Aunt Bee's limbo party. Honestly. Does she have to wear that humongous hippie shirt, it might as well have her age emblazoned on the back."

"Well, he's not so young either, is he?"

They watch as he lifts a stray lock of hair off their mother's face, leans in close as if to kiss her, then in the most elegant maneuver, pulls her close to him, keeps dancing, cheek to cheek.

"If the men we knew acted more like that, Suave, do you think we might like them more?"

"All I know is Mom deserves this."

"Deserves what? Happiness in the form of a movie star in her bed? Suave, I swear you cook like a damn old person . . . if I hadn't just quit, I'd be puddling this out to my cultists tomorrow morning. Dessert time," Prell sings, carrying two goblets of Pudding in a Cloud, layered stripes of Cool Whip and chocolate custard.

Suave and Prell leave Nora and Eduardo sitting on the couch, digging into their puddings, to disappear into Suave's room where they climb into the size fifty-two men's houndstooth pants, each wriggling into one leg, then yanking over their chests the red Mr. Roger's cardigan that manages to endow them with one giant, mashed-looking boob.

Down the hall and into the living room they lurch, Prell first, Suave a leg behind, Suave first, Prell catching up, singing in their highest mice voices:

It's a beautiful day in this neighborhood;
A beautiful day for a neighbor;
Would you be mine? Could you be mine?
Won't you be my neighbor?

While Suave and Prell improvise their silly Stuckey's routine, Nora laughs and laughs, openly adoring her girls. They mean the world to her. Time would tell with the dashing and handsome Eduardo. But for her daughters, old issue of her flesh, Nora will prove faithful to the end. Loyal to these high-spirited young women, her replacements, the truest romance of her life, Pearl Marvel's longest, most enduring story.

The Widow's Poet

ora Bettinger arrived late to teach her first class at the university. A newly published poet, she was taking the place of a nationally recognized writer who had suffered a nervous breakdown. Nora questioned what could be so emotionally ruinous about teaching; didn't schools offer amnesty, a routine as fixed and narcotic as her last marriage had been? With that life taken from her, no one was more astonished than Nora to find her decline into grief broken by the near-merciful net of artistic accomplishment.

The poetry workshop was held at night, at an hour none of the permanent faculty was willing to accommodate. But nights for Nora had become cruel, each presenting itself as a formidable liaison with an unwise, engulfing solitude. Besides, she thought it pragmatic to avoid the hot, cerebral pitch of a university in daylight, best to ease her way in, come more gradually to terms with what might well be her new, regulated life. Toward the end of her phone interview, the department chair hinted to Nora the possibility of a tenure-track position, if things (and this was vague) worked out.

Nora's husband, Harlan, an oncologist, had been dead nearly two years. She was hardly desperate for money, though her income was not as secure as she had been led to believe; at his death, Harlan left debts unveiled to her by a somber team of lawyers, a regrettable portfolio of overseas investments gone sour. Nora also hoped for something to stop this newest silence from bricking her in, something to start her writing again. Her only book of poems was nearly three years old; published to respectful acclaim, marginally reviewed, then quickly, considering the time it took to write them, forgotten. She had written nothing new, certainly nothing that felt dangerous or vital, in almost two years. With Harlan gone, her world had stilled, grown sarcophagal. She was only forty-eight years old but in some major, horrible sense, her future seemed finished, literally unimaginable.

TO NEUTRALIZE HER PANIC, Nora chose a black velvet skirt and black jacquard tunic, black cowboy boots with a red star bursting across each heel. She wore a lipstick called Sorceress and loosely plaited her waist-length red hair. Almost negligently, Nora cultivated a poet's persona, perpetually distracted, narcissistic, disorganized. She favored rare, expensive fabrics, vintage clothing tossed together in a haphazard style her husband had affectionately but nonetheless condescendingly referred to as fairy-tale chic. Throughout the year it took Harlan to die, she had worn a series of antique Chinese jackets, boxy and loose, with floppy linen pants and round-toed, silk-embroidered Chinese slippers. For reasons that had kept her in therapy most of her last marriage, Nora could not accept how lovely or capable of sustained accomplishment she was, how highly regarded by other poets. This could be said to comprise her charm, a modesty largely specious since its source was self-hatred; it also caused low-grade suffering, a chronic malnourishment of what was now too blithely and perhaps overdemocratically called the soul.

She'd moved to Phoenix from Santa Fe, quickly selling their home in Tesuque, featured three years earlier in a summer issue of *Architectural Digest,* when Harlan was still well enough to deceive her. After a brief stint teaching at Santa Fe Community College, partly to pay Harlan's debts, she'd accepted this sudden offer as a visiting professor and—not without resentment and some curiosity—she had moved. Instead of acclimating, Nora found herself unabatedly lonely. For the first time, she became alarmed by her own will-lessness, the gutted-out feeling ominously resident in her. So the evening of that first class, with the September air unseasonably hot, like cooked felt, holding every smell and oppressive, she walked twenty minutes late into her assigned classroom, B 216. Were they the same everywhere, a conspiracy of classrooms, unchanged since her own student days, the glacial spines of fluorescent light, lifeless walls the flaccid color of scraped potato, the dead, deliberate-seeming ugliness?

(She would believe her camouflage a success until he surprised her one night, saying he had recognized it, her drowning panic. "It was the way you turned to close the door," he said, "not wanting to shut yourself in with a blank pack of cards like us. You were scared as hell."

"I was that obvious?"

"No. But I see who you really are. You could say it's my gift.")

Nor had she anticipated that teaching would so exacerbate her loneliness. Caught within the collective gaze of thirty-five students, pinned under the glare of their blunt, privileged assertion—"look, I've paid for this class, purchased the right to stare as long as I please"—and gaze too mild a word, Nora felt stripped by such cool, communal regard. Eventually she would get used to it, learn to deflect, but she realized it was not only the late hour that made this class unpopular with faculty. The room held a demoralizing, immiscible combination of graduate and undergraduate students, serious writers as well as students seeking refuge from seriousness. The class was a bureaucratic compromise, an unsettled sabotage no one liked, not even the students. Nora despaired enough after that first class, consisting mainly of coerced introductions and an explanation of the revised syllabus, to flip through the calendar in her office afterward (where she had announced she would be available for two hours before each class), to count the weeks remaining in the semester. Thirteen.

For the second class, she changed her preparation, hoping to jump-start their interest. And it had gone well enough, she thought, the students seeming to like her, some even joining in on a spontaneous discussion about finding a balance between writing from the heart and adhering to the discipline of craft. She told stories, bits of gossip about various now-famous poets she had studied with years before, including a goatish, monocled old British poet whose proposal of marriage she had nearly accepted just to be able to live in England. Only one dark-eyed young man had sat there, stony, stubborn, with an acid, malefic gaze. Volunteering nothing. Scowling. When she got home that night, there were two messages on her voice mail. One from the English department secretary, asking her to please drop by to sign some papers, the second a male voice. "Tonight was bullshit. I hated your class."

Dream

—Dismissible, surely harmless, this young man who approaches me. His interest not sexual. Trusting his presence, I lie down a moment—where, on what?—Abruptly he leans over me, brings a heavy iron mesh to rest over my face and neck, his hands lock around my stemlike throat.—

"You looked hungry last week. I brought you this."

He unwrapped and split apart a turkey sandwich; suddenly there was a small picnic on her mostly bare gray desk. He ate rapidly, with undisguised appetite, drank Coke from one of those absurdly oversized convenience store cups. Nora peeled a white leaf of turkey out from the bread, refused the potato chips. She felt self-conscious, eating in front of him.

"It was you who left that phone message, wasn't it?"

He laughed. "I shouldn't have done that. I'm so embarrassed. I just hated that class."

"Why?"

"I don't know, it was that crap—excuse me—about writing from the heart."

"You don't agree?"

"No. I shouldn't have called though."

"I'm not used to teaching." She was about to add "and I'm no good at it"—but perhaps that was not fair. Mainly, she was new. In need of reassurance. "How long have you been writing poetry?"

"I haven't. This is my first class." He laughed, slid a handful of pieces of candy across the desk. "I have a bad sweet tooth. All's I have in my apartment is ice cream and candy."

"I adore chocolate."

"Here then." He slid across more of the miniature, wrapped chocolates. "To keep in your desk."

He began to wait for her each week, sitting on the floor outside her office. She would unlock the door, while he stood behind her. She would sit in her chair, he would sit in his, the desk between them, a smooth, grave island meant, she supposed, to represent authority. She hated the desk, considered having it removed, bringing in a sofa, coffee table, chairs. Or perhaps nothing at all.

He was, she guessed, in his early twenties. Each time, covertly glancing, she was surprised by how handsome he was. His skin was a rich oak color, his black hair curled, clung to the nape of his strong-looking neck, his eyes were the dark seditious brown of horses, an assassin's eyes. His physical appearance, of which he seemed mainly careless, suggested an urbanity that collided with his boyish lapses of grammar, his high, goofy laugh splitting into an otherwise smokey, alluring voice. Everything about him held her deepest attention, alerting her to something crouched, muscled and glittering with hunger. In conversation, he was by unpredictable turns naive and brilliant, schoolboy polite and brutish. Easily excited, he spoke explosively, his words diving over one another, lost in a hot, rapid blur of speech. As a species, adults bored Nora, their codes too easily pierced, their actions largely governed, even overruled, by habit. Christian was mercurial, his moods capricious. She made a mental list of his qualities as if they were symptoms, as if symptoms served some purpose. Soon she expected him to show up outside her office, was irritated if another student legitimately (these were, after all, her office hours) interrupted them. One evening he wasn't waiting outside her office, his chair in class was vacant. When she got home, she checked her voice mail, but the light was dark. Unable to sleep that night, Nora attempted to shame herself with an unflattering comparison to the aging writer in Thomas Mann's "Death in Venice," lethally enraptured by the gray-eyed Polish boy, Tadzio. She felt no sympathy for herself, and yet, he was the first person since Harlan's death who made her feel capable of both joy and argument, it was as simple and, given the circumstance, as potentially sinister as that. Her therapist once suggested Nora feared humiliation more than disappointment. She supposed that was true, but had no idea why. Too rarely, she found, did epiphanies born of analysis guarantee change. One simply became more conscious of an ingrained faultedness.

(FOR MONTHS ON END, Harlan had not come near her. For years, because they could afford it and because they had agreed on the necessity of privacy in a marriage, they slept in separate bedrooms. At the end, he was solicitous of her comfort, generous in a calculated way, as if to buy off any suspicion of his increasing inability to love her. She grew too tired to care, told herself to take the high road, found herself wondering if a child of their own might have made the difference, a cliché, but weren't clichés weak variants of truth? Would family life have helped keep Harlan, what was that ridiculous word, happy? Or worse, content? His childlessness was the single great sorrow of his life, he said, not offset by her two grown daughters, whom they rarely saw, who belonged, he claimed, to another time. Fantasies of a healthy marriage to an undepressed man were recurrent, crucifying. Yet since his death, Nora had come to see how his sort of love had shielded her from some unformed part of herself, kept that potentially monstrous part walled off, how his own inability to love had, ironically, kept her safe.)

ON THE DAY she made up her mind to ask Christian if he would go to the symphony with her, Nora stopped at the English department, as she had been asked, to sign some papers. The elevator stopped, and she began to step off when she saw him sitting outside another professor's office, his back to her. She stepped backward into the elevator, jabbed the button to shut the doors. Panic followed an icy thought—what if he routinely (obsequious little brownnoser) chatted up all his professors? After all, their talks had been mostly about writing, his desire, her experience. He offered impassioned opinions grounded in a violent contempt for anything less than sublime. He constantly lamented having read so little, compulsively purchased books, mostly poetry and biographies of poets, and always (since he was poor) on credit. She had read one of his poems; he had brought it to her, then agonized over surrendering it. For her sake, Nora hoped it was trite or average, that it would underscore some flaw of immaturity—but its sophistication of form and the agility of language stunned her, and her resolve to keep him at a distance, to instinctively defend herself, completely gave way.

————

AS SHE UNLOCKED her office door, he stood behind her, apologizing. Family troubles, he said. For the first time, the space across her desk seemed penetrable. Christian looked morose, heavy, brooding, his black curling hair a little oily-looking. Perhaps he wasn't as good-looking as she'd made him out to be, as she had imagined in the richness of his absence. She noticed the slightly broad nose, the eyes somehow smaller, less lustrous. Unexpectedly, these imperfections emboldened her.

"I'm going to the symphony this Saturday night. Would you like to go?"

"I'd love to." His eagerness was artless, relieving. The phone rang—she excused herself.

A student, calling in sick. Nora looked up, caught him regarding her mouth in a way that made her feel languorous, drugged. While she was still on the phone, he wrote her a note, pushed it across the desk and left. He would borrow his sister's boyfriend's car, pick her up around seven.

HE ARRIVED a few minutes early. He had dressed tastefully in a thick gray wool sweater, corduroy pants, good black shoes. His hair was so clean it glistened. He opened the car door for her, complimenting her—almost unintelligibly—on "looking nice." He drove fast, talked more rapidly than ever, got lost several times. When they narrowly avoided a collision, her response was serene, even amused. "Poets are catastrophic drivers, you know," she smiled over at him, thinking yes, death would put a convenient—if exaggerated—end to her dilemma. In the dark, pocketlike intimacy of the car, she listened to him talk about his day, a rushed, almost compulsive spillage of events from someone who could have been, in terms of his age at least, her son.

INSIDE SYMPHONY HALL, they were shown their seats and given programs, which they diligently paged through. She wondered if people were looking at them. Why would they? Christian was utterly intent upon the program notes. She was a mother, an older sister, an aunt. As the house lights darkened, the conductor stepped to center stage, bowed to acknowledge his applauding audience. As the opening movement of Mahler's *Resurrection* began, Christian leaned forward in his seat, elbows on his knees, hands locked under his chin, in a rapt trance. During the intermission, as people moved past, he neither spoke nor looked at her. He sat staring at nothing, the way he often had in class. An almost adolescent thought occurred to Nora— was he a genius, perhaps mad? After the intermission, as the hall darkened, he sat forward again. During the second half of the symphony, she tried hard to hear the music, did hear but was distracted, casting sidelong looks at his feline profile, the breadth and solidity of his shoulders. Her blood felt silken and hot, her limbs loosened, her breath dug into her heart. After years of Harlan's scarcely touching her and only when she'd asked (nearly pleaded), she believed herself asexual, neutered. Now greed swept through her. Looking at his hands outspread on his knees, she felt depraved and utterly grateful. She felt like a character resurrected from her old romance-writing days, when words meant money, not art, to her. Meant food on the table.

After the concert, they remained in their seats, the very last to leave the auditorium. Silently, he deferred to her in everything. Outside, they sat beside one another at one end of a broad set of steps leading down to the sidewalk. Concertgoers passed them on the stairs, conversing, laughing; Nora and Christian sat facing a pair of mud-brown, dispirited horses harnessed to an empty, black-gleaming carriage.

WITH HARLAN, going to the symphony, to the opera or to a play had been a cerebral exercise, dispassionate, dispatched with analysis. Were she with him tonight, she would have walked straight past herself, not recognizing the diminutive woman in the long bell-shaped white skirt and maroon velvet jacket seated beside a dark-haired brooding student. She and Harlan would have been among the many affluent older couples heading on to an expensive restaurant or to someone's home. But Christian responded to music the way she had been made to feel ashamed of and so had kept hidden—for him, too, it was a violation to fracture silence prematurely, to descend too quickly into the heaviness of speech. They sat until everyone had gone, until even the horses, exhausted and moving as if on a tide of retreating memory, had borne their passengers off.

She spoke first. "Are you hungry?"

"Yes," he said. "I haven't eaten all day."

This time, he drove more expertly through the city. He showed her his old high school—a Jesuit school for boys—Brophy Preparatory Academy.

"It's gorgeous. Spanish colonial?"

He shrugged. "I'd like to live here, with the priests."

"Why? Do you want to be one? A priest?"

"Christ, no. I want to corrupt them."

AT AN ALL-NIGHT RESTAURANT, he chided her for only ordering toast and coffee. She watched as he ate a cheeseburger, french fries and a vanilla milkshake. He told her he and a friend used to work at a Burger King, after that they'd cleaned bathrooms at resort hotels where one of their jobs had been to pour ice into all the freshly bleached toilet bowls. He was the oldest, he told her, of nine. His mother was from Mexico, his father was Irish Catholic, an army officer. His mother took art classes at a small college in Alabama where they'd been transferred. There were a lot of problems in his family, he said, but didn't elaborate. She'd come from a military family as well, Nora told him, attending a Catholic girl's school, an only child. Her third husband, a doctor, had died of cancer. They'd had no children together. (How bluntly pruned, one's life, all its green anguish broken off.) Their conversation was awkward, tentative surges of intimacy followed by cool retraction.

———

HE TOOK HER HOME, waited until she was safely inside before driving away. In her bedroom, with its unadorned taupe walls, Nora undressed and stood before her round dressing-table mirror. The room itself was monastic—all her things in storage—only a crucifix nailed above the bed was wanting. As she observed it, her body—dull white fish, hidden veins and arteries a jeweled, gnostic map—Nora suddenly remembered he had never asked for directions to her house.

HE NO LONGER stopped by her office, had dropped out of class. And when she checked, his name was not on her class registration list. Still, he didn't call, so one night, she phoned. A male voice, not his, answered. Against a background of loud music, the voice yelled for Chris, not Christian, and she heard him laugh, though it didn't sound like him. Confused, she started to hang up.

"Hullo?"

"Hi, it's Nora."

"Oh, hi. How are you."

Cold, so cold sounding. She wanted to drop the phone, it was branding her. He said he was sorry, he had to go—his sister and her boyfriend needed a ride—she could hear, thought she could hear, the sister's boyfriend—taunting Christian—did they know, all of them, did he ridicule her?

Oh my God. She vowed never to call again. Two nights

later, he called. They talked past one o'clock, how they would live in Mexico for the summer, travel by train, rent a house by the sea, read aloud to one another on its vine-shadowed porch, write. The next night she called and he answered, cold, taciturn. When she questioned him, he said he just got that way sometimes and no, it wasn't about her. But she believed it was. Curtly, he accepted her invitation for dinner that Sunday, then said he had to go. Sunday morning, while she was out buying flowers, wine, chocolates, he left a message—he was sorry, but he had to go to a rosary for an uncle who had died, one of his mother's brothers, he would have to go for the next nine days or his family would murder him. Playing the message back, dragging his voice for what—what lie was she dreading—Nora dimly realized her danger.

DRINKING THE WINE she had bought, or most of it, gave her the idea to call and leave an elaborately enunciated message for the Irish professor—insufferably blank little man—that she'd be delighted to see him for dinner. (Proving neither the remedy nor distraction she'd hoped, the man was a study in chauvinistic blight; when he asked to see her again, she refused openly and ungraciously.) When she returned, there was a message from Christian asking if she wanted to go to the opera. "See," she said aloud, "cultural companions. My boundary, plain as day." After which she sat up late, rereading his poems, new ones he had given her in a wheat-colored folder. Exceptional, each one roused admiration striped with jealousy. He had never asked to read her work, an offense she interpreted as flattery, clear implication that he liked her for qualities beyond her obvious gifts. He had read one poem, published years before in the *New Yorker*, a poem she had used as an example in class. He didn't care for it, he later told her, hated poetry that hacked the world into clever precincts. No one had openly criticized her, and after the initial shock, Nora found the experience seductive. She saw his criticism as a means of overpowering her, but since she did not agree with it, with his opinion, his aggression was harmless—it induced, contrarily, a giddy, combative vitality.

Dream

—At the university, I stop outside each of three black doors running the length of a corridor otherwise resembling a colorless tumbrel. I take an elevator down, its doors open onto a claustrophobic, mouse-colored hall where I walk through a doorway with a set of open wooden steps descending into a basement. To the right of the landing, deep in soft ash, a small piece of white clothing is dropped. A man stands beneath the open stairs. I step back onto the elevator. It shudders horribly. I am standing inside my own steel shroud—

"When you die, how do you want it to be?" He asks casually.

Nora remembers her big, antique bed in Santa Fe, its lace-covered pillows, the table with its vase of queenly white delphinium, music, a green view, hospice workers, morphine. "I suppose I would want to be pampered."

"That's ridiculous."

"Why? What's wrong with that? How would you choose to die?"

"On a street, among strangers, in a lot of pain. What's the point if it's not horrific? For a while, I used to walk out into streets, try to get hit."

They are in her parked car, after having been to a disappointing production of *Othello*. This time, he had not wanted to stop anywhere, but had driven her car, fast, recklessly, back to his apartment. All Nora wanted was to be in bed with him.

"Are you going to invite me up?"

"No. I don't let anyone into my place."

"Never?"

"Only my sister, sometimes with her boyfriend. I don't even like them in there."

"Why? What about me?"

"I don't know. It's just private. Plus it's a mess right now."

"What if I said I desperately needed a glass of water?"

"You lie. You don't need a glass of water. You can wait till you get home.

"Christian."

"What?"

She took a deep breath, dived. "OK. Can I say this? Yes, I can say this. I'm attracted to you."

"Me too."

"You're attracted to me?"

"Mmhm."

"God."

"What?"

"I'm old. Well, older than you."

"How old?"

"I can't tell you."

"Oh c'mon. Say. How old are you?"

"How old is your mother?"

"I don't know. Forty-two."

My God, she thought, I'm older than his mother.

Then he said her age as if he knew. "You're forty-eight."

"Does that bother you?"

"No, but I probably shouldn't take classes from you anymore."

"Why? Oh. Well, maybe not."

"These things never work out for me."

"What? Relationships?"

"Yeah. And to be fair, there's something else. I'm not exactly sure about my sexuality."

"Oh. Well." Suddenly Nora went from seeing herself as his unorthodox lover to his elderly aunt and long-toothed confidante. She tried retrieving herself. "Who is? We'll go on being cultural confederates. That doesn't have to change. God, I feel embarrassed."

"Why?"

"I guess I'd been wondering if we'd be lovers."

"I've wondered, too." Before he got out of the car, he leaned across to give her a stiff comradely hug. She drove home, entered her apartment, its blank walls, the ghastly chrome furniture, none of it hers, none of it anyone's. She went over to the phone.

"Christian."

"Hey." He sounded amused, tender. Why did his voice intoxicate her? Maybe she could just sleep with his voice.

"I think we should sleep together."

"I don't know. Maybe."

"I'll drive back over."

"No."

"I could bring you back here."

"No. Besides, I don't sleep in beds. I sleep on the floor."

"You mean on a mattress?"

"No. I mean the floor. On the bare floor."

"With a blanket?"

"Yes, with a blanket. I move around to different areas."

"Like a dog." Nora laughed though she was definitely aroused by the image of him asleep on a bare floor. "Sorry, I didn't mean to be insulting, it's just that you made me see a dog. Let me come get you."

"What about afterward?"

"What do you mean?"

"People get emotional. I hate that."

"No. Maybe I just want to lie next to you or something."

"You mean you want a good hard fuck."

"Just hold you, see what happens."

She heard him yawning. She was boring him. He was bored.

"Forget it. It's an insane idea. I'll leave you alone."

"No, I'm just really exhausted. And I have to stay up, I've got two papers to finish and a novel to read by tomorrow."

On her kitchen table were her student's poems, their papers. Unread. Across the room were her own poems. She was writing again.

"I'll talk to you later, then."

NORA DROVE UNTIL she sat looking up at the lit windows, at his walls, bare like hers. She drove home, drank half a bottle of red wine, swallowed some herbal sleeping capsules that smelled like dirt, lay facedown across her bed, all the lights in the apartment on.

NORA STRUGGLED TO CONCENTRATE on teaching, on writing. She made amends and went out twice more with the Irish professor, led him to believe she enjoyed his company, went to someone's house for dinner, agreed to a Christmas trip with a casual friend from Santa Fe, a ten-day Mexican cruise. She wrote four hours a day. She had her teeth bleached, her nails manicured, got a massage, a facial, joined an aerobics class, bought clothes and a great many pairs of shoes at several vintage shops she found. Every night she noted if his window was dark or the curtain drawn back; sometimes standing out of sight beneath his window, she heard music—always violin (Paganini) or piano. The afternoon she received news that three of her new poems had been accepted by a prestigious literary journal, she called.

He seemed glad to hear from her, though he made no mention of the two weeks of silence. "We should celebrate," he said.

"Tonight?"

"I have to go to my aunt's tomorrow, actually for the whole weekend. When I get back."

"How about Christmas shopping together and dinner afterward?"

"Good Christ, I've got so many people to buy presents for— all my brothers and sisters, both my parents, my cousins, aunts and uncles—and absolutely no money." He was laughing. "So. Nora. Your poems. What are they about?"

"You."

"That's flattering. Or is it? I'll have to read them. I think my new boss really likes me. He's taken me to lunch three times this week, and yesterday, he insisted on buying me sixty dollars' worth of poetry books." Christian had a part-time job at a local bank.

"Obviously he likes you."

"I guess." He laughed. "The not-so-good thing, though, is he's 'married,' and his husband or whatever lives with him. They own a gorgeous house out in Paradise Valley, plus a bunch of places in California. He's invited me to stay in any of them, for free, whenever I want."

"Christian, the man wants you."

"You think? Should I have let him buy me those books?"

"How old is he?"

"Late thirties maybe. Old."

"Thanks."

"What? Oh, for crying out loud. I don't think of you that way. As old, I mean."

She hated this conversation. "Gifts have their price, that's all." She decided to counterattack. "I've gone out with that Irish professor a few times. He calls every day."

"Have you slept with him yet?"

"No. He has no idea how unappealing he is—he reminds me of a bad menu. If I ask you something, will you be honest?"

"Am I still attracted to you?"

"How—"

"Because whenever you're insecure you ask."

"Can you come over? I miss you."

"It's late, Nora. I'm tired. I'll call when I get back from my aunt's. Plus I have to finish the de Sade book. Did you know he only had sex with people he thought ugly? He claimed it made the act honest."

Dream

—Night. In my car, driving to his apartment. My body feels extraordinarily keyed up. I follow him into a half-lit space reminiscent of an old-fashioned laboratory. He stands so close I smell the foul, putrid odor of his rotting teeth. He is cloaked in a substance translucent and glistening, as if sealed in whitish spittle. Lifting up his arms, two bladelike wings unfurl, giving him the ominous, slightly wet appearance of an insect. There is a moment's erotic suppleness, an impression of threshold, then his eyes narrow, his countenance turns malignant as he engulfs me in the viscous dirty white wings, suffocating and entrapping me. I am given to understand the enchantment, the tainted lure he put forth of sex so that he might seize the source of his lust, my life.—

Though her world was contracting, becoming ever more still, Nora found no will in herself to rise out from the paralyzing undercurrent. She kept all her shutters closed, preferring semidarkness. She slept late into the afternoons, ventured out at night, refused what few invitations she received. She read, wrote, taught class, some of the students liked her, some didn't, she hardly cared. She understood she should be socializing with faculty members, her colleagues, accepting their invitations, arranging a little get-together at her house. Getting those who counted to like her. Pleasing her students so their evaluations would be favorable. She should be doing all this in order to be asked to stay on, in order to attain the privilege of a so-called grown-up life. She thought of resuming therapy, it had been more than a year, the longest she had recently gone without help. The black, flickering drag of his voice held her under. To an extent, Harlan, guarded and pragmatic, unimaginative but kind, had anchored her to normalcy. Without him, some pernicious value had wakened, an ineluctable craving for a young man who wrote of bloody dismemberment, of sexually inflicted humiliation—she had elected him her newest messenger, her elusive, maimed twin.

He was sitting outside on the steps as she drove up. A maroon baseball cap, turned backwards, made him look younger than he was. They had not seen one another in three weeks.

"Hey, Nora. I've done something crazy. I've been bad."

She could tell it was sexual, the nature of his badness.

"I met this actor who gave me a front-row ticket to this musical he's in—*Showboat*—I went out with him after, then he asked what it would take to get me to go back with him to his hotel. I said—it was just a joke, really—a hundred dollars.

Without a word, he put a hundred-dollar bill on the table in front of me. So I did it. I let him give me a blow job. Now he's calling every ten minutes, whining. Jesus. It wasn't even worth it, the whole thing was pretty pathetic."

"When was this?"

"Saturday. I thought of calling you. Then, oh sweet Christ, last night he shows up at my apartment weeping and crying, sitting on my couch saying he's all in love with me and what was he going to do and would I fly back with him to St. Louis for his next show."

"You let him in?"

"I had to. It was raining like crazy and he was outside my door, crying. I felt sorry for him. So I listened and then he left. I felt like his goddamned therapist. And that's not all. Today my boss asked me to go to San Diego with him. Plus he bought me a really nice watch."

"Christian."

"I know. I've been a whore all day. I'm going to give that other guy his money back. He kept saying he'd pay me a hundred more if I let him do it again."

"Would you?"

"No. I felt like laughing. He was so . . . into it."

But Nora heard his pleasure and, yes, guilt, yes, the need to confess, yes, confusion, but overall, the pleasure of being desired. She understood the abasement of these men, their pridelessness. After all, she had been buying Christian dinners, symphony and opera tickets. Yesterday she'd ordered an Italian leather jacket for him. She shared their new mad hope.

"I don't know. What can you live with? What your church or your parents taught you? What you would do if God were watching? Whatever the hell you want? I have next to no advice to give you here."

"I cannot believe I let him do that to me for money." Christian gave another of his unsettlingly high-pitched giggles.

In the shopping mall, a garish Christmas wonderland, she realized they had only been together at night, in dark cars, in the shadowy back booths of all-night restaurants, in darkened concert halls. She was shocked by how tired he looked. How unwell.

"Do you have a list or something?"

He dragged a crumpled index card out of his back pocket. He wore a dark green baggy sweatshirt, black corduroy pants, black shoes—he'd left his baseball cap in the car and his black hair was slightly flattened, tangled. When she put her hand out for the list, he snatched it back, mumbling, "No, it's mine." He wandered, almost shuffling, from store to store, fallen into one of his dead zones where he would not talk or respond to anything she said. The air around him felt stale, the word *demonic* strangely occurred to her. They floated, revenants, in and out of shops where nothing drew his notice except a dagger, a poster of Ophelia drowned, a man's black velvet jacket, an hourglass. In one department store, he collected an armload of blankets, saying he should buy one for everyone in his family. Then, dazed, he put them back. She had given up suggesting things. Exasperated but still hoping to tease him into a better humor—after all, Christmas shopping was supposed to be fun—she stuck an empty gift bag she'd found on a bench into his hand. He went on walking, as if unaware it was even in his hand. As they moved through the mall, Nora noticed several men glancing at Christian. One particularly striking-looking older man turned to prolong his gaze.

"I'm starved. I have to eat something." Nora veered into the nearest small restaurant, sat in the nearest booth. She was being rude, but he was worse. Maybe he was traumatized by his recent sexual congress, what he'd discovered himself capable of. She hadn't bothered to see if he had followed her. But when she put down her menu, he was sitting across from her, a partially contrite look on his face. Over yet another of his tedious hamburgers—that was all, besides candy, she had ever seen him eat—he confessed he was too exhausted to continue. "I'll wait until I get home for Christmas, my sisters always help me."

And what, he asked (clumsy attempt to molify her!), were her plans over the winter break?

Other than a cruise with her newly divorced friend, and a brief visit to each of her daughters, both of whom had married and, strangely, moved back to Illinois, Nora had no plans. Aside from Christian, she had made no friends in Phoenix. Several weeks ago she'd imagined going with him to Rome for Christmas, but his family was possessive of him, though she guessed they knew little enough about who he really was. She had assembled a hostile family in her head, a mosaic based on blood riddles he had told her . . . the pig they slaughtered every Easter, how he and his cousin pinned the sliced-off ears and tail to their heads and asses and took out after the shrieking girls . . . his uncle's dog, how he had dreamed of sticking a knife into it, holding the dog tight in his arms so it could not struggle as blood flowed from its chest . . . the Buck knife he had found in the garage when he was three years old, what he had done with that knife (he would not tell her, nor would he tell what terrible thing happened at a church youth retreat, so terrible he had to be sent away to live with relatives for a year) . . . puzzles or bits of puzzle left for her to connect and solve. Now Nora watched him carve a Styrofoam cup into long blistering curls, using a small knife she had never seen before. Watching his skillful hands, his fierce expression, an awareness overtook her that sex was not what he wanted, it had never been what he had wanted from her . . . she saw clearly, as the knife sliced coldly on and on, he wanted her death. He sat silent in the darkened restaurant, ignoring her, working the knife. Courting her, not for sex, less for her poetry, wanting the bright release of her blood, skin split like fruit, a hot, gutting death in his arms. Her sexual heat, her desire for him grew so unbearable, as if in secret acknowledgment, Christian suddenly stood and walked quietly past, the knife still open in his hand, not looking at her.

"ARE YOU GOING to invite me upstairs?"

"OK."

"You are allowing me into your place?"

"Not for very long."

A couch, midnight blue, heaped at one end with books and papers. The blanket he had described, green-and-black plaid. A flat, yellowing pillow with no pillowcase. A small kitchen table and two chairs, the kind that came with an apartment, much like hers. Taped to the wall above the table, dozens of handwritten lines from poems. Rilke, Mandelstam, Trakl, Tsvetaeva, Plath, Baudelaire, on and on. Slender towers of poetry books rose un-evenly off the floor, dozens of larger, less graceful books covered the floor, the counter, the table's false wood surface. He showed her the drawerful of chocolate bars, the mint-chip ice cream in the freezer, literally all he had to eat. A half-empty liter of Coke. As she stood in the small kitchen drinking tap water from a red plastic glass, Nora saw he was trembling. "I'll just drink this and go," she said, then realized she had to use the bathroom.

The bathroom was dark and neat—toothbrush, razor, generic shampoo, a blue towel on the floor. Coming out, Nora noticed the door to her right, because Christian stood, militant, outside of it.

"Your den of horrors?"

"My space," he said vaguely.

He followed her down to her car. He reminded her of a big, lumbering dog or bear. Some animal heavy with itself, stubborn, defined by its burdens.

Unlocking the car door, she sighed.

"What?"

"Nothing."

"It's something. Tell. You have to tell."

"You can't laugh. Promise."

"I won't."

"I want to kiss you."

"OK."

First letting her into his apartment, now willing to be kissed? She turned to face him.

"Christian. Good God. You look as if you're about to be bloody hanged."

"Sorry." He stuck his arms around her waist, his face expressionless, his eyes staring off somewhere.

After a second's disbelief, she touched her lips to his. Pale, chaste, dead.

"That was the weirdest kiss of my entire life."

"Why?"

He was sincere. His whole body was rigid.

Nora quietly rested her head on his shoulder.

"My God."

"Mmm?"

"You smell incredibly good." A little dizzy from the smell of him, she reached her hands to the back of his neck, played with the curls of his hair.

"I'm losing my hair. My hair's falling out."

"Really?" I have a friend in New York, a playwright, she's half bald and strides around the streets transforming shame into magnificent style. Men adore her."

His arms were still clasped like cold staves around her. She buried her head deeper into the thickness of his shoulder, the deliciousness of his scent. Swooning, that would be the exact word for how she felt, but could never admit.

"I'm falling asleep." He yawned.

"I think we should have sex sometime."

"Not now."

"I know, but sometime?"

"OK."

"My birthday's next Friday. Want to be my present?"

"Sure."

Nora was roaming around outside her body, having heard herself just ask a young man to be her birthday present, hearing him say yes but not very enthusiastically. It seemed she was now a person who would say or do anything to have sex with a gloomy, cryptic young man she scarcely knew.

NORA RESTED HER FOREHEAD on the steering wheel. She had asked for what she wanted and he had said yes. Even the bruising dread of Christmas was lifted. They would exchange gifts, write letters, cherish the same books, he would call late from his parent's home (she saw these parents as ogres, enemies who would be scandalized, would despise her, if they knew). While he was away, she would visit each of her daughters, come back, volunteer at a children's hospital or homeless shelter, she would call up those faculty who had tried befriending her. She would be happy because she was loved. Possibilities bloomed in Nora so forcibly she wept.

WEDNESDAY, TWO DAYS before her birthday and because she had heard nothing from him, she called.

"Hey, Nora. Remember that actor? I sent his money back to him in St. Louis. And I had a good talk with my boss, I told him I couldn't accept any more books or other stuff from him." Christian talked a little more, pleasant, self-contained, preoccupied with exams, papers, applications for graduate school. He hadn't even asked how she was.

"My birthday is the day after tomorrow."

"Wow, that's great."

Silence.

"Oh, our night." He laughed. "I forgot. Can you believe I forgot?"

She thought she was going to be sick.

"Oh no. You're mad. I can tell. You're mad, aren't you?"

"No. I'm not."

"Yes, you are. I'm sorry. Maybe it's just that we planned something that should be more—spontaneous."

"I have to go."

"Hey, I'm sorry."

Silence.

"Oh no. Now my sister's here. She's taking me out for dinner. She had another argument with her boyfriend. I have to go."

(TEDIUM, HARLAN COMPLAINED—no one had forewarned him of the tedium of dying—a monotony burst into by flagrant, meteoric pain. During that last weekend at the hospital, and this was possibly the worst thing Nora had done, she sat by his bed while he slept and did nothing, absolutely nothing, when a small grease ant, looking meticulously fashioned from fine black wire filaments, labored past Harlan's chin, which she had earlier shaved for him, crossed one corner of his lips and climbed deliberately up into one nostril. She should have reached over, brushed it away—any decent person would have—but she did not. Aware of the vengeful spite underlying her fascination, Nora allowed the insect to make its journey into her husband.

The worms crawl in, the worms crawl out
The ants play pinochle on your snout . . .

She sat by his bedside another hour to see if it would emerge from one nostril cavity or the other. It did not. Even at Harlan's funeral six days later, Nora imagined the ant still in him, the first to colonize and consume, once her husband lay deeply punctured into the earth, sealed over, unable to assail her with his indifference.)

LATE THURSDAY NIGHT, when Nora was about to take a bath, he called. "I'm just not going to be able to meet with you tomorrow night, I'm swamped with homework and finals, I still have to do all my graduate school applications, I'm completely freaking out—I haven't slept in four days."

Her disappointment—or rage—was so clotted, it blocked her voice.

"Look, I know you must be disappointed."

"You said you'd be with me on my birthday."

"Well, can't you make other plans?"

"I was counting on . . . you."

"Oh, now you sound just like my mother. Look, I could try to stop by after I'm done at the library. It might be kind of late, and I can't promise."

She hung up, waited. The phone did not ring.

NORA DROVE HER CAR up over the curb, parked sideways beneath his window. Tripped up the steps, banged her shin. *Fuck.*

Fuck him. Bastard. Asshole. I hate him. With her forehead pressed to the door, she raised her hand, beat her curled fist against his stupid always-shut door. Turned, slid her back down along the door, sat on the concrete, knees drawn up. It was midnight. Her birthday and because of the harsh gold bundling of light around her, though she couldn't get to her feet, she knew the door had opened, he was there.

"Please."

Had she spoken? A light shudder passed through her. *Frisson,* she thought.

"Old bitch." She could barely hear him. "You really need it, don't you?"

What she felt first in her belly, a hot numbing rush, then between her legs, the spiking terror and excitement, rendered her so weak, he had to lift her, haul her *(stupid cunt)*, pin her arms, kick shut the door, lock it, turn off the overhead light, push-step her into the room she deserved but had not yet worked hard enough to deserve, no different from the rest.

He let the last of her clothing fall to the ashy, stained carpet before his eyes narrowed and he caught up her nakedness in the filthy sheet ridden with the yellowing lice of ghosts, the telltale shiver signaling she was his.

—How quickly recognized, her hunger, the same as the rest, its crude, revolting cry—childhood's long whip driv-

ing her into a union with pain she will name sweetest of pleasures—her need had been greater, her loud wail uglier, was all. Until I found her, she lacked an executioner. Until now—a poet!—she lacked proper imagination. So let my stranger's art, its languishing rituals, its practiced techniques, its degradations, begin.

Her Last Man

There was a time—the girl being ten or eleven—when she refused sleep, would not shut her eyes until she had been saved by an imaginary physician, a gentleman whose face bore the look, jejune and anguished, of a poet.

In what way does this concern him: Old Teaser, Torment and Tickler, Ancient Warrior, Mr. Thorn in Her Girlish Hide? What does the black-cloaked Englishman with the quality of mercy have to do with HIM, that snoring heap, that nose shrieking whatsit she stood over each night, as if her small pointed stare might ever shut down his loathsome eruptions? Indeed, he waked one night to find her little aspirin of a face hovering half an inch from his; well, what she was scheming was how to shave off his nose, just to have some peace. So the girl held her glowering watch while his wife, head pricked with sponge curlers, slept, dead to the world on his other side.

D. D. D. L.

Now it happened Old Teaser, Torment and Tickler, etc. demanded to be called Dearest Darling Daddy Lover (D. D. D. L.), most particularly when she was forced to supplicate, to wheedle and to cozen the skinniest of permissions. In turn (and never did she know why), he called her Jaz. Her handprinted birthday cards, the gold-glittered tags on his Christmas gifts were obediently marked in this way. "For D. D. D. L. Love Jaz."

IN THEIR HOME where such gifts and cards came and went, was an upstairs den, dusky harbor of D. D. D. L.'s psychical life and kinetic energy. The den, as any fool can guess, was off limits, verboten—thus did the child trespass, snoop with no small nubbin of excitement, dig in her heels before the four profane mysteries: CARDS, COINS, THE BLUE WOMAN and some RHYMED POEMS (a trail gone cold, skinny spoor of lead). There were rows of law books, too, bricks of dry blood, justice bricks, and model planes, Navy fighters, so gray it ached to look at anything but their honeyed seams of mucilage. Furniture, was there any? There must have been, but furniture was not what she was after. Not one stick mattered, so all the sticks, all the furniture, remained invisible.

The child had her sunnier playtimes. Though she wasn't sure what rape was, not precisely, she flicked her pink Madame Alexander dolls like sticks, no, like flint against one another to get a spark, thinking yes, this was what rape was or anyway some close approximation. Afterward, she "cooked," smashing gumballs of Wonderbread on her silver-painted radiator, a gray stuff for dolls which she herself swallowed.

THE CHINESE EMPEROR

It is October 1926, and Morris Stoddard, eight years old and not yet stricken by polio, is taken by his mother and father to see China. It is a melancholy autumn, full of pent-up clouds split by sullen, flickering stamens of lightning. One afternoon, which mimicked in its plumlike atmosphere night itself, Morris was seated between his parents on a train steaming its way through Manchuria, when a magnificently costumed entourage of persons crowded in from another car—a gorgeously hued, greedy-eyed packet of birds desiring only to bring this boy before the Emperor, who sat seven cars up, disguised as a rice farmer and complaining of chronic ennui which, for this entourage anyway, could prove dangerous. Wherever little Morris was taken in China, whether by train, by blood-red rickshaw, on foot between his parents, he caused vehement waves of sensation. He was gawked at, prodded and poked, venerated. His hair spun like milky filaments of glass around the extraordinarily round ball of his head. He possessed a set of wide-apart, jarringly blue eyes shaded by a triple set of ghost-white lashes. In Peking, in Hong Kong, in Singapore, on all the roads and pathways in between, little Morris was a sight, a diversion fit even for the jaundiced gaze of an Emperor whose entire life thus far seemed to him to resemble nothing so much as a brief waking paralysis.

HOW THE DOG PROFITS

She is to sit without moving as long as it takes, all night if that's what it takes. Hurting no one but herself. She cannot leave the table until her plate is clean. Abetted by the family dachshund, George, who bloats, sturdy as a frigate, releasing meaty gases beneath her chair, she will instruct herself in the low magic of making food turn small, smaller. (Her two daughters will become wastrels, wasters of food. Half-eaten, it will add height to bedposts, turn bacterial yellows and venereal greens behind sofas, under hutches, in closets. She will feign disgust but in fact, by such rot and squander, be made ferociously, inexplicably happy.)

A STINGING HAIR-KNOT

Winter nights, she is thrashed at gin rummy. Three games, six sets, two out of three. The trophy is on a bookshelf in his den. Silly, made of cheap plastic, it fits perfectly in her hand.

Summer evenings he wallops her at Ping-Pong. Three games, two out of three. Would he let her win one time, just to see how winning feels? No, the little trophy keeps to its den through all those games, hundreds of games, it is never excused, nor does she excuse herself from its power.

When she sits deep in the eye of his wide, trousery lap, he whirls the hair on her forearm, whips it into a mercurial stinging knot before wrestling her down to the silver carpet, then trumpeting, a hunter, into the tender white band of her midsection—old boar face, old javelina—until she whoops for mercy, until her ears nearly burst.

The godhead bristles, the bristles spiny gray jabbers. A head like a sea urchin. She stands behind his orange chair, rubbing the jabbering godhead with its oil of Vitalis. He is too big to be approached all at once, you must concentrate on one aspect at a time, like a god. Respectfully massaging the scalp, she cannot remember his teeth.

She can point out the best girls, the ones worth honking at. From inside the aquarium light of D. D. D. L.'s pink-and-white Ford, her eager-to-please eyes fix on the passing world. Even today she can spot beauty, his kind of beauty, faster than any man.

GENTLEMAN OF RESCUE

On her back in the upstairs hall, the girl catalogues the world's woes. Perishing in a second-floor hallway as her parents, downstairs, read the evening news, she feigns delirium, is death's prize on a street deep in snow-rimed filth. Then the round whipping of carriage wheels and she recognizes his footsteps, gives herself up to the tall, cloaked figure. Eyes closed, she is lifted, enfolded, carried off to his bed. It is her bed of course, and in it she arranges herself in a second crucial posture—that of being revived. The Englishman in the woolen cloak, his lodgings are plain, he is, she supposes, handsome, his skin glints like veal, his breath is redolent of sweet clove, he sets a wooden chair by her bedside, carries spoonfuls of salty broth to her lips . . . days pass, she gains strength and a waxy, foreign charm. The tableau labors toward the inexpressibly sweet moment when the young and no doubt handsome physician, still in his cloak—it seems he never removes it—inclines his head to kiss her. With this, she falls asleep though she will wake hours later to scout the house, both upstairs and down, for fire . . . a terror she has—of being burned alive.

BROADS AND LIVING DOLLS

Look at the pair on her!
That doll is really stacked!
Gina Lottabosoma, what a beaut!
Deal the cards, daughter . . .

not those, not the ones with fifty-two white-skinned women on their suit faces, not the queen of hearts, bare-boobed and sylphing like a dolphin out of a red heart-shaped box, not the ace of spades, naked except for a velvet top hat, spike heels with net stockings, one arm saluting, an arrested angle of motion. Naked women, lightly tabbed with paper-doll outfits—British sailors, Spanish dancers, French maids, Santa's helpers, college coeds (why not munitions workers, fruit pickers, slaughterhouse workers, meat packers, chicken pluckers, seamstresses?). She shuffled them, made kaleidoscopic gibberish of these commanding officers of her sex.

The coins, silver dollar–sized and made of light aluminum alloy, had more naked ladies on them. These images were less interesting than the cards, though their texture was appealing. She would rub the cool bumps, press on the declivity between . . . lick the breasts, finding them telluric and bitter.

And what about Blue Woman in her square frame of honey bamboo? The Hawaiian with her South Pacific hairstyle, features reshaped to Caucasian tastes, hand floating up to secure a hibiscus bloom in her luxuriant blue hair? Her chalky breasts overtook half the picture space, the face a bland speck compared to those blue papaya breasts. Here was a woman who never bought a man packs of underwear at Montgomery Wards, never washed and sorted that man's socks, never fried a panful of pork chops the way he liked or didn't like, never took issue with him, never nagged. Blue Woman would not grocery shop or iron dress shirts, as she was learning from her mother to do, collar first, then cuffs, then sleeves, then the broad, billowing backs. Blue Woman held some privilege, would never be made to iron his linen handkerchiefs, those monogrammed nose flags, as she was, again and again until each of the twenty was perfect. The college poems were cornball, saccharine plots to run away to Tahiti, to lounge and loaf. They did not match the gruff, emotionless act she knew in his dark brown suit; they did not match the gray-trousered bristler she accompanied on Saturdays to the hardware store, coming home to stand in the driveway, hold the two-by-four as he sawed, pinch the flat-headed nail between forefinger and thumb as he slugged it with his hammer. His poetry repelled her more than his law books, uniform and ugly, more than his insectlike warplanes. It was his cards, his coins; it was flesh she returned to, revisited, in her itch, her worry, her fret to understand.

Lady of Spain I adore you!
Lie on the floor
I'll explore you.

THE COW PALACE

. . . a draughty poorly lit convention center built on a landfill along the southern edge of San Francisco Bay. The drive was always the same. She would stare out at the metal hinge of a bay, no radio, no talking, just breathe in and out, his air hers, his air hers, bay-water hinge. And as if waiting until she was well-hypnotized by all the nothingness, his hand would crawl over, grab the tender flesh above her knee, pinch hard as he made a squawk-squawk sound. She would yell, shocked back into the confusion of her body. She hated his doing that, wanted to yell "quit," but the inequality was severe. Inside the Cow Palace, where there was not one cow, she went to car shows, boat shows, small-plane shows, holding his hand through the long, machine-smelling labyrinths of cars or boats or planes, male amulets of flight, escape, speed. Bored silly, she would collect free brochures or eat her lunch, a steamed hot dog cuffed in damp waxed paper, a Coca-Cola in a waxed red cup. Card-deck women in sequined bathing suits and spangled boots draped themselves, the skins of exotic animals, against the hulls of boats, the hoods of cars. She felt it redundant to point them out to him. Surely he had eyes. Instead she worked to hold the slippery brochures, sorting them by size or color, the only girl among throngs of wistful men at the Cow Palace bumping up close to what eluded them, a sequined tango of shining women and vehicles of power. A thousand cash-lined corridors, a thousand trompe l'oeil exits, a thousand glimpses of what they would never have. There is some immense sadness hidden in all of this.

HEADS

Fishhead
Fathead
Lunkhead
Knucklehead
Chowderhead
Hammerhead
Meathead
line 'em up against a wall and shoot 'em.

—D. D. D. L. utterances

As a child, I believed my face, maybe my whole head, was ugly. Have I mentioned that?

(point to the child's knee)

You know why an Indian doesn't have his kneecap here?

WHY?

Because he has it on his own knee.

(hold her hand)

Did you know you have eleven fingers?

I DO NOT.

Ten nine eight seven six. Give me your other hand. One two three four five. Six plus five equals eleven.

OH.

(command her)

Five hundred times before you come out of your room.

IWILLNOTSAYSHUTUPTOMYFATHERIWILLNOT-SAYSHUTUPTOMYFATHERIWILLNOTSAYSHUTUPTO-MYFATHER Without checking to see she had done the full five hundred (which she had), without knowing what she had learned or if she had cheated (she had), he took the bundle as if it were the configuration of sin itself, raised high the metal cymbal of the trash can, dropped her lesson in.

DUMBCLUCK. Skirting the obvious. What? That you ratified yourself as ugly? Stupid to the core, a fool to the quick? That you could spot beauty in women and present it to him? To D. D. D. L. . . . another stacked gal, Love Jaz. The warnings of memory are fierce. How to distinguish memory from revenge? Remembrance is a bald, gloomy ball of string that refuses to arrange itself into anything useful or good. Oh illuminate your homely monument with one true and perplexing thing:

> "A recluse named S. S. Stambaugh for several years collected EIGHT-INCH LENGTHS OF STRING from a local flour mill in Tulare, California, and by knotting and winding the pieces was able to build a three-foot-diameter twine ball in less than two years. Upon seeing the huge creation a friendly visitor calculated that STAMBAUGH HAD TIED 463,000 KNOTS IN NEARLY 132 MILES OF TWINE TO MAKE THE 320-POUND BALL. (March 22, 1938)"

A POOL OF STRING

At thirteen or fourteen, in the dying center of those difficult years, she helped him map out a swimming pool in their grassy, thigh-shaped yard. A cotton string vibrated six inches above the yellow-green stubble, connecting stakes thirty inches apart. On the other side of their redwood fence was a Christian cemetery. She watched the feet of the dead, their shoes scattered like blackened seed among the graves, watched their sly, glittering feet nudge under the shallow rooted fence, itching to get at the rumor of a pool. She splashed around inside the stringed-off area as if the grass were deep, wet turquoise, wondering how pool water got to be blue if the plaster itself was white, or was it painted blue, no, she didn't think so. The string pool took up most of their mottled, Italy-shaped yard, OK by her, no more pushing the mower in stout, mortified shoves, a chore that somehow made her hate herself. On windy days, the string thrummed like some white aeolian harp, its shape that of a lima bean. Kidney bean, he corrected. She wanted to ask why pools had to be in bean shapes at all, who decided such things.

Their pool stayed until the string slackened and the stakes fell over, and winter grass needled its way up. Then one day, a windy, buffeting day, she followed him out to take it all down and couldn't find a polite space to ask why.

(D. D. D. L.'s dreams rose swiftly, marking hers with indelible, foreign imprints. The time they were to move to La Spezia on the southern coast of Italy. The travel brochures, the complex itinerary, plans snapped down like postcards on the kitchen table night after night, she read her own life by those cards. She watched herself invite classmates over to swim in her new backyard pool, staving off their rejection of her. She was a schoolgirl in Italy, walking by the sea. Her dreams stood like acrobats on the shoulders of his. After the string pool disappeared, after La Spezia vanished, both forbidden topics, after he no longer loved her and she did not know why, when there was a vibration, a nothingness between them worse than that of the neighboring dead now made to wear the trim of dog turds she hurled over the fence, those drab medals, troweling them up and flinging them high over the fence with a racy anger, with a thrumming rage, here you flat-on-your-backers, here you voiceless army of experience, take this and this and this.)

LEGS

When she was a baby, her feet stuck like rosy jujubes to the high brown loafs of his shoes. Music could play, any music at all, as he led and she followed, stuck to those shoes, stuck like glue. But by thirteen, dear Lord, she couldn't help disgusting him, and it was then he made up the Sunday lesson. Her splay-footedness (she walked like a duck and only sometimes remembered to turn her feet until they were straight as pins like everybody else's), her legs tatting up like shabby laces, duck feet rattling like loose dice, her whole body a thickish bog of embarrassment. By sheer ineptitude she tried to escape, but no, he always insisted she try again; he put the same music on, planted his arm around her waist, imprisoned her hand as he said: "Now look, you. Relax. The man leads, the woman follows." She tromped on his shoes, or tripped over them until his wife, as if on cue, minced out and oh, Miss Mitzi was really good. The coquette in her twirled right out, the girl of twenty. Meanwhile the lummox was marched forward to repeat herself, speeding her disgrace to arrive sooner at that moment of his disgust which meant—yippee—free for another six days.

Relax? Relaxing had nothing to do with his fox-trot, box

step, rhumba, swing, his tango. Spins she braced for, always spinning the wrong way, galumphing into him, or at the outer limit of the twirl couldn't find her way back and stood there, hangdog. It was at the hangdog part she slunkered off to scrub the burnt roasting pan, a trounced Cinderella. Then the right two danced. The two who had been dancing for years now. Did the lummox set forth the disturbance that made him desire his wife again?

At neighborhood parties, he danced with and kissed every willing woman there. And they all were, willing. Our lummox hunched against the wall, plastered herself to the sidelines, mute, black-green with jealousy. How many of them knew, as she did, about his right leg, deformed by childhood polio? But the leg, draped in elegant trousers, the leg didn't matter. He spun other men's wives, twirled them like tops until their faces blurred and shone up at him.

Simpering cow-ballerinas. She thought them fools.

The Sunday lessons stopped, he spoke even less except to ask what was she, non compos mentis? When she came down out of the trees, he said, he would talk to her. She had no idea what he meant. To her it would be a reward, a vacation, don't you see, to vanish into the black, leafy dens of trees, to leave her legs forgotten on the ground below.

LAST MAN

Long after she had slept with all the men she imagined she would ever have the strength to sleep with in her lifetime; when it felt as if it were winding down, finally over; when she quit the game she could not seem to win—what do men want though they themselves cannot say?—now as she paired up her white stumpy soldiers, her painkillers, and laid herself down in an absence not to be confused for sleep, Buddhist tapes droning in her ears—empathy is true morality—loss, loss, loss—when in her bed a finely tuned stillness prevailed, broken only by the occasional water-murmur of hope; when it had become this, D. D. D. L. moved home, well, moved nearby. At the first news, she swam back and forth in the swimming pool: back and forth, panicking up and down the rungs of an invisible ladder (she has her pool now), howling beneath the water. At last the woman grew quiet, remembering her bell-like Buddhist tapes, the voice which spoke only of forgiveness, of loving kindness, of the moment.

Then D. D. D. L. suffered a heart attack which quickened her to his side, made her honest. Love you Daddy. He sat on his old orange throne, afraid to stir, afraid of that fraidycat thumper, that meaty knuckle in his chest. Recover, each of his doctors chided. One day, out to get the mail, wearing the T-shirt she gave him for his birthday (For D. D. D. L. Love Jaz) a philosopher's shirt:

To do is to be—Socrates
To be is to do—Plato
Do be do be do—Sinatra

he is struck by a speeding car, shot like some white and fading bullet over the hood by a woman who claims she never even saw him, where in the world did he come from? He is a big man, wearing a philosopher's T-shirt. How can she not see him? He has always been everywhere.

At his feet, trying to hold a cushion of frozen peas to his swollen ankle, she gets him to smile with a joke she overheard him tell years before (What did the elephant say to the naked man? How can you possibly breathe through that?). The peas don't work and he needs her help. He asks to be undressed and put to bed.

HOW WOMEN MOURN

First play the nurse, still in your black knit dress, put the old poet to bed. On your knees, untie his laces, tug off his long black shoes, not the ones your bare feet stuck to, stuck like glue. Undress him in a raw nerve of glory (Red-and-green-plaid boxers!). It is an Art, this undressing of an old father, an art which evokes pity and some covert delirious hope.

At the bedside, he breathes hard, in some undefinable pain he insists will be cured by lying down. Turn down the covers. Your father's uneven legs against the sheets, legs that danced, that haven't danced, you see him naked. Before you is a giant taken down, an aspect at a time, like a god.

When his pain worsens, pull him up by the arms to wait on the edge of the bed. Three rescuers, the same ones who earlier had picked him off the street, now lift him out of the house. Through the ambulance window, his hair-hanky, his flag of fading white hair, his profile so like a boy's, whatever became of the bored Emperor of China?

THIS DOCTOR IS a callow fellow, his skin bad, his pants drag like wilted lettuce around his cheap shoes, what can he know? Father! my statistic, my dull sentence from a medical text, old warrior, old teaser, old tormentor, thorn of love in my childish side.

When you recover, D. D. D. L., and I have made them say so, I swear to do this one thing:

Herd into your hospital room all the women I can find, young, old, fat, thin, they're all pretty, you see that now, don't you? I will drag in my daughters, who will be sick at the sight of you, you on the threshold of it all, wearing such unholy weather, I will march them in, sacrifice without mercy. "Sing," I will command the older one. And she will. She will sing like Marilyn Monroe, a breathless, living doll singing "Diamonds Are a Girl's Best Friend" and "My Heart Belongs to Daddy," while the other one, like me, too much like I was, sits sullen and hard to please in the corner, nosing through the pages of fashion magazines. Yes. Day after day, I will order women to fill your room, demand that all the nurses be pretty, may the world be restored, may my powers tell you beyond all telling—the other men were as nothing, they are gone. I have dismissed them as I always meant—or was I taught?—to do.

He flirts weakly, barely speaking or moving, winking at the afternoon nurse who doesn't suspect she is the dyed-blond shield I shake before death who, we all know, is fairest of them all.

I lose him, regain him, lose him, regain him—what sport this turns out to be, no trophy at the end, was this what he meant—lose to illness, win to nurses, lose to illness, win to nurses. I tell you, I will put each nurse to bed with him. I will lay me down beside them. I will fit us all—sardines!—his wife will float above, her fists full of money and rain, the bed piled high and wide with all the women I can find so he will be hidden from that weary scavenger, death. (For D. D. D. L., Love Jaz.) I am standing on the orange chair, watching you grow bigger not smaller under the weight of so many beautiful women now that you understand (for I have made you understand) that all women, all of us are beautiful. You, my first and last man, for whom I am fearful and proud.

No one showed me the five highways to your failing heart. Boats, cars, planes, women. I have traveled all but this last—

still I am with you, determined to be there, flying forward, circling wider and farther, wherever we go, neither leading nor following. Look! A woman dancing, reassuring herself, ready, letting go her father's brave, thin-as-a-playing-card, see-through old hand.

Funktionslust

Copulation is the lyric of the mob.

—BAUDELAIRE

Happy gorillas are said to sing.

—JEFFREY MASON, *When Elephants Weep*

Up and down the dull coastline of her desk, Eleanor Stoddard ticked her fingernails, Minnie Mouse airbrushed onto each bismuth-pink shield. She was back from Ladies where she'd flattened out *Newsweek* from its bug-swatter twist to read about the chief of the Cloud People, his vow to leap off a high cliff if a certain foreign petroleum company purchased his tribe's ancestral land from the Colombian government. Who would want that sort of thing on their conscience? There was a stamp-sized photograph of the chief, pudding faced, with black, beveled hair and the sexy, charismatic gaze of the not-quite-holy man. His story sat to the left of another article (both were recipe-card sized), about world forest fires and greenhouse temperatures, beside a pink graph nobody would leap off of anything for. Flags—not math—inspired sacrifice, thought Eleanor. With her Disney nails, she sliced out the Cloud Chief's small story, not wanting to lose his heroic possibilities. This was the second bit of news sparking the dry foolscap of her afternoon. The first was the gorilla, recently delivered to her garage by a young ecoterrorist, Moser, now airborne, leaving Phoenix for a week's walking tour through Cluj, a medieval city in Romania—at the sudden behest of his newest lover, an aspiring historian named Boris.

At the tether end of her forties, Eleanor lived alone. A former aspiring actress, Nora Stoddard; housewife, Mrs. Evanston 1983; former romance writer, Pearl Marvel; and sparsely published poet, Nora Bettinger; Eleanor had worked six years in this auto-collision inspection station, an exotic bloom turning brown around the edges, potted into her gray cubicle. Her one window allowed a mean view of a spinach-colored hedge and, beyond, the diminished rear ends of a McDonald's and an urban dairy. Six years dragging her pink nails over clients' paperwork, outlining where and when to take their cars for repair, handing over fat checks based on Rorty's estimates. Unnerved by their collisions, clients grabbed at their checks until Eleanor reminded them it was for repair, for vehicular damage, then offered a consoling peppermint along with a customer satisfaction card. She had won the Employee Recognition Award six years running, tallying the highest number of positive remarks, never mind they were mostly about her smile, her legs, her hair or, like the retired fireman wrote, how she was a dead ringer for Reba McIntyre, as if that would make her drop like a stunned fly into his bed (which it nearly did). Eleanor hammered all six of her awards onto the spongy gray wall, in a circle, like a clock, around her Mrs. Evanston photograph. That contest had been years before, and recently she felt it, that she was coasting, picking up speed, going downhill. The sex-kitten rigamarole, the glam-o-rama, the I-enjoy-being-a-girl mind-set, the sequins and folderol, where had it gotten her? Where, for instance, was Mr. Right? Moser's answer was biologically terse. "It's secretions," he would rant, "secretions and scent. Take any woman who smiles and ovulates at the same time—no question—she'll mow the men down." "Baloney," Eleanor shot back. Now she wasn't so sure, plus she was finished ovulating, so where did that leave her? Flailing about in a crisis she couldn't identify. Dragging open the file-cabinet drawer, she raked up a tangle of fried calamari with her nails, ate it, formed a squadron of green Tic Tacs, then flicked them into her mouth with her tongue. She did this to keep from screaming, to keep from jumping off the squat gray cliff of her desk.

In the waiting room, a tall, long-bellied man paced with his cell phone, shouting in German. Behind him was a jacked-up white van with Rorty, the inspector, standing underneath the dented portion holding his clipboard. Eleanor once asked Rorty, at an office party, if he ever worried he'd be crushed. Biting down on a bacon-wrapped chicken liver, he'd winked—*only by my wife, sweet thang*. That's who she worked with, had to jack her own life up above and keep it there, in the clouds. For the first two or three years, Eleanor tried livening things up around the holidays, wearing leprechaun hats to work, Santa suits, Easter bunny ears, green makeup and a witch's pointed hat. One year she gave everyone—even Rorty—a personalized Easter egg. For close to six months, she'd written and posted a Daily Inspiration on the announcement board and nobody said a word. When she ran dry of inspiration, everyone complained. Lately, her thoughts kept contracting into one shrill, pinpoint ambition: find a husband. She'd never found the right one; now she kept her list of Eligibles under the inflatable Mr. Potato Head anchored to the far corner of her desk. She'd won Mr. P. at a party for her friend Rhoda, whose current husband drove a Frito-Lay truck. They had all gotten drunk and played potato games, peel the potato, find the potato, roll the potato, etcetera. Mr. Potato Head, a door prize, had detachable Velcro trimmings, an orange beard, felt glasses, a red turnip-shaped nose, lips, ears. Everyone except Eleanor had wanted the other door prize, a Mr. Potato Head vibrator.

He was not her only inflatable. In her bedroom closet, stashed behind a tiered rack of athletic shoes (until it disappeared in a gas explosion, pelting the strip mall with a clunking blizzard of white athletic shoes, she'd worked two evenings a week at the Strapless Jock), Eleanor kept a blow-up security guard, a gift from a Turkish journalist who became concerned, even panicky, about her living alone without a gun, an alarm or Mace, not even a dog—undefended!—a woman with her hair, smile, legs, etcetera. On his way back to Ankara, he'd ordered the security guard shipped to her from an airplane shopper catalogue. Eleanor had never bothered to inflate the man, who resembled Burt Reynolds right down to the five o'clock shadow; he was still doubled and tripled over in his clear, soft plastic bag. She sometimes thought it might be nice to have a complete assortment of past lovers and husbands, puddled into plastic bags like so much dry cleaning, ready to be inflated, strapped into the passenger seat of her car, seated in the wing chair by the picture window or made to stand by the stove—deterrents, tall male balloons planted like mines. On her fiftieth birthday, she could inflate them all—hooray!—her bloated village of nostalgia, starting with angst-ridden, myopic Victor Leipzig, when she was seventeen, to now. Now was different, though. Eleanor was considering "closing up the lab" as Rhoda called it. Until she met Moser, who'd seen three of his ex-lovers cremated and was only twenty-six, the whole thing hadn't seemed real.

Hilton, a juvenile gorilla, had been slated for AIDS research in a local university laboratory. He was scheduled to be injected with the virus, given experimental treatments and combinations of drugs, to live out his short, tortured life in a small, gray cage (familiar enough, thought Eleanor). Moser intended to release Hilton into the jungle he had been captured from, but now, in the middle of his rescue project, because of love's abrupt seizure, he had flown to Romania.

The world, it seemed to Eleanor, had shrunk to the size of a cocktail napkin. Claustrophobic, excessively connected . . . Moser's was a green, ecological awareness intended perhaps to morally refresh, but Eleanor felt suffocated, like being part of somebody's big, nosy family. Okay. She picked up Rorty's call. *Five minutes 'til my guess-timate, sweet thang,* he said, adding that the cell-phone German with the weirdo skinny braid was on his way in to see her.

Right after he bought the Harley, Moser couldn't sleep. He kept running down from his fourth-floor apartment to make sure the black-and-salmon bike wasn't stolen. When he told Eleanor he was thinking of sleeping on the gravel next to it, holding a pistol, she told him that was silly and gave him her spare garage-door opener. She'd never ridden with him on the bike, but one night, wearing only her Disney World T-shirt, she'd sat on the Harley, playing with the black, beaded fringe on its handles, like a kid on a ride outside Wal-Mart. That night, when she pulled into the garage, Moser's bike was in its usual spot, but when she opened the door, she caught what had to be the gorilla's rank, blunt smell. Then she saw the metal cage wedged between her suitcase and a neat stack of Pine Logs. (To gain sympathy, Moser'd told her countless animal horror stories like the one about the chimpanzee, rescued from a birdcage that had hung ten years in a dark garage.) A purple box of dog biscuits sat on top of her suitcase, a yellow note taped to its side. Were the biscuits his? What if he escaped when she opened the door to feed him? Should she tell the German man when he showed up to take her to dinner that Hilton had been spirited out of a laboratory the night before, that she was an accomplice—not to mention a sitting duck—now that the actual thief was in Romania, in Cluj, what kind of name was that for a city—it sounded like luggage. What was the reason Moser couldn't wait until after Cluj to steal Hilton? Leaving her—fool!—holding the bag? She couldn't remember. Eleanor crouched down in front of the cage.

"Hilton? I'm here. Eleanor Stoddard. Your hero, remember Moser? went away for a few days. I don't want you to worry. See?" She pointed to the yellow note. "Instructions."

The gorilla regarded her gloomily—almost cynically, it seemed to her, before shifting to turn his back. The fuschia metal tag punched into his left earlobe gave him a disconcertingly punk look. For some reason, Eleanor thought of the Patty Hearst kidnapping, how the Symbionese Liberation Army had kept Patty in a closet, only letting her out to rob banks.

SITTING NAKED and tailor-fashion on her floral chenille bedspread, Dieter (like *tweeter*) Heinrichs unbraided his hair. Two Apache women had dyed it for him. He sounded as if he was bragging as he gave the blackened hair a vain, girlish toss. "And *Funktionslust*? Ah," he sucked air through his gapped teeth, a wet, sensual sound. "It means taking huge pleasure in what one does best, enjoying one's abilities."

"What a word." Still fully dressed, Eleanor emerged from her closet, where she had rushed to hide her Affirmations board. On this board was a list of qualities she sought in a husband: dark, virile, cultured, emotionally sensitive, loves opera, oral sex and pink bubble-gum ice cream . . . she'd been drunk when she'd made the list. "So what are you good at?"

"Oh, that's easy. I find all of (*suck*) life so beautiful. I find you (*suck*) most incredible of all."

For pity's sake. Wow. He was certainly corny, but so pleased with himself, with his funny hair and long soft tummy, she decided, sure, make love with this man who told her he was an adopted Lakota and knew a lot of Indians, knew them really well. Dieter Heinrichs, physical therapist turned cultural entrepreneur, regularly flew Indians to Germany to conduct sweat lodges and feather circles. Maybe he would take her, too? Was he an Eligible? she wondered. Not after he'd complained that monogamy was a negative "thought frame" interfering with his *Funktionslust*. "Nature is my model," he'd proclaimed, "and she is too clever for monogamy's straitjacket."

What was it about Eleanor lately that turned normal conversation into a monologue, with the other person doing all the talking? When he ended his philosophic chat with himself, Dieter Heinrichs took so long singing the praise of every curve of her as he uncovered it (much like the time Eleanor thought to prolong Christmas by taking an eternity to unwrap each of her presents until her parents, Mo and Mitzi, both shouted at her), he was forced to wake her up by the time he'd gotten her completely nude. Napoleonic and noisy, Dieter *funktionslusted,* exuberant and gamboling, carnal as a child. Then he fell asleep, a pink snoring starfish, a probable monster who, eyes closed and mouth open, looked incapable of harm. On her hands and knees, Eleanor crept around him, felt a faint, fickle sense of endearment as she studied the pale, relaxed umbrella handle of his penis. She wasn't tired anymore. Her house felt charged up with two males in it, one here on her bed, one caged in the garage.

Not wanting to wake him by flushing the toilet, Eleanor went into her backyard to pee behind the blossoming, poisonous oleanders. Back in the kitchen, she stared at his shoes, at his fringed, butter-colored leather jacket with the red and black beadwork, at the cell phone on the table beside the jacket (throughout the evening he had made a series of rambling phone calls in German). She stared at his shoes so long and so suspiciously, she began loathing them and by extension loathing him, the raw-looking starfish in her bedroom. All at once Eleanor knew a man could be laid bare by his shoes. These were light brown skidders, sliders, slippery, sloppy rundown roadsters, big and nasty looking. The nasty-looking shoes spoke, saying she'd better be a sharp cookie and look through his wallet which lay under the cell phone. The trifold wallet fell open to a snapshot of his wife and three children tricked out like Indians—odd, as if she tried to be German by wearing lederhosen—like the year she was six and wore her Annie Oakley costume, cap guns included, every single day. Then she heard him cough, a phlegmy smoker's cough, and, quick as a wink, shoved the wallet back under the phone. His teeth were bad too, crooked, stained, gapped. Shoes and teeth. Lord. The evening was losing its dignity. Time to check on Hilton.

He was wilted on his side, asleep. What's my *Funktionslust,* Eleanor wondered. What's his? Retreating to the kitchen, she swallowed two times the recommended dosage of Celestial Seasonings sleeping pills before flopping down on the living room sofa to mentally review her Eligibles. Discounting Dieter (married, dyed hair, bad teeth, telltale shoes), and disqualifying Moser (homosexual, twenty-eight, the closest she had to family, a sort of nephew-son combination), left her with:

1. Gub Mix, the Christian plumber who'd answered her ten P.M. emergency call and stayed until 2 A.M. When he started talking religion from under her kitchen sink, his legs splayed like blue cornstalks across her linoleum, she admitted to having had a vision of the Virgin Mary where Mary foretold she would one day give up all she owned and travel south. This pushed Gub's one button. Sliding out from under the sweating pipes, he asked permission to pray

over her, then cupping his grimy hands over her head, prayed long and loud while she stared at the black rubber bell of the plunger. Gub had heavenly blue eyes and a squashed-in head. His head made her think of a square gift-box bashed in on one corner, but she refused to ask questions. When he was ready, he would explain. Last week he dropped off a pot of miniature yellow roses and a double CD of Christian rock music.

2. George Dorsey, the Mormon who showed up to empty last year's water out of her swimming pool. She'd sat by the side of the slowly draining pool, swinging her bare feet while he brushed clean the plaster sides of the pool and told her increasingly off-color stories about people he'd met on his mission in New York City, like the man who had sex every Saturday night with his wife's dog, a blond Afghan. George spoke humorlessly about "pumping iron," and his muscled skin was so tan, Eleanor imagined chomping affectionately into his thigh would be a lot like sinking her teeth into a hollow chocolate rabbit. What worried her, though, was his vehicular rage. Driving her home from a lunch of Chinese dim sum, he'd become agitated, hurling grapefruits out his window at offending cars. And reaching down for her purse, she'd encountered an aluminum baseball bat under the front seat. So when he kept calling, asking her to one of his

church dances, she stalled, telling herself that for a Mormon man as handsome as he was to still be unmarried, something must be drastically wrong.

3. Duke Ruff taught TaeBo part-time at a community college, part-time at the Ak-chin Casino. He lived out in the desert in a trailer the color of dead daffodils, stuck up on cinder blocks. He had no shower curtain, and like a fool, she bought him one, installed it herself, then made her prized osso buco before discovering the pile-up of unreturned casserole dishes in his broom closet and realizing how many other women had tried to win this man with desperately competing casseroles. In bed, he said the same thing over and over—*it feels like you and me've done this 150,000 times before*—and she never knew what to say to him except maybe he'd worked too long at the casino.

4. Doc Sparkles, an eighty-nine-year-old millionaire, married five times. He played squash on Tuesdays/Thursdays and wanted her to fly to Puerto Vallarta with him, then go on a Russian cruise. She'd met Doc at the El Charro Lounge one night, where he'd rambled on and on, his talk vortexing like a tiny tornado up into his stained cowboy hat. For now she kept that flirtation barely going, the dimmest of embers.

What did Gub, George, Duke and Doc all have in common? Loneliness? She should get up from the couch right now and call Mose in Romania. Use the German's cell phone, let him foot the bill. Wearing nothing but her fluorescent Tweetie Bird slippers, she changed her mind and stood cooling in front of the open refrigerator, munching on a handful of Hilton's salad mix. She swallowed three more pills and thought of women she'd read about in certain societies (she couldn't remember which ones) who, when their hair turned gray, were allowed to touch all men, women and children with impunity. She remembered a friend of hers, a film developer, describing medical photographs of a sixteen-year-old girl's ovaries as a series of botanically succulent O'Keeffe paintings, then saying how a single photograph of a sixty-year-old woman's ovaries looked like a sentimental illustration of death.

She peeked in on them—on Hilton and the German— then, woozy from all the skullcap, passion flower and valerian root, clamped her headphones on and lay naked on the floor beside the CD player, falling asleep to *Cosi fan tutte*, Mozart's cheery, inane libretto.

The very next night, with Dieter gone to his powwow in Sedona, Eleanor woke from a hugely perplexing, erotic dream. Before bed, she had changed the sheets, lit her pumpkin candle and lavender incense (Moser claimed studies showed men consistently aroused by the smells of lavender and pumpkin) and fallen asleep with her headphones on, blaring a tape about intuitive awareness. As she lay in the dark, the fan paddling above her, she dreamed that a small, dark ape climbed on top of her and began to fuck her, his penis small, glistening and quick. Waking up in a state of lubricious excitement, she yanked her now-silent headphones off and sniffed. Overwhelming the mix of lavender and pumpkin was a thick stripe of smell, rank, almost scorched. Attaching her reader's light to her forehead like a miner's lamp, Eleanor followed the smell, tiptoeing out to the garage. There he was, in the crown of white light cast by her lamp, asleep, his salad hilled in the corner of the cage, bleached and dingy looking.

Why not let him out? Surely he was intelligent and sensitive, more so than Dieter, who had called three times already, leaving breathy New Age messages, powwow drums thumping in the background.

Pensive, Eleanor shook out a fresh panful of salad for Hilton while listening to the Three Tenors—Pavarotti, Domingo, who was the third?—when the phone rang. Answering, she heard a distinctly alto hum from the garage.

"Eleanor?"

"Mose?"

"Hey. I'm stuck here for a while."

"What?"

"Yeah, I'm sorry."

"But—"

Stealthily, the portable phone to her ear, she opened the door to the garage. Hilton was thrumming his fingers along the cage mesh, eyes upturned, his guttural hum charged with a sorrowful yearning; she actually lost track of what Mose was saying from his end in Romania.

". . . what can I say, I'm in love—with Boris obviously, but with Cluj, the Romanians, the air, the trees, the sinks, toilets, toothbrushes, trust me, dog shit smells divine here . . ."

The CD ended, the house a tomb.

"Enough, Moser. It's biology, right?" Her voice startled her so she lowered it. "Look, I'm happy for you, and I can handle it."

"Ever-awesome Eleanor. I have a sudden wish to marry you. How's our man?"

"Ah . . . good. Really good. I'm not sure he's eating enough. Listen." (Here she shut the door to the garage and whispered.) "The truth. Can he undo his cage thingy?"

"The latch? Absolutely. I trained him as part of a contingency plan. Then again, I've never seen him do it without heavy coaching. Why? Did he get out?"

"No. I don't know. I'm not sure." Eleanor whipped open the garage door to see what he was doing. Nothing. Plinking through his lettuce. "Does he like music?"

"Oh yeah, Hilton adores opera. It makes him kind of sing. Why? It sounds like you two are hitting it off."

Though his back was to her, Hilton was listening, she knew it. "Would it be okay to let him out? I think he's getting bored."

"I don't know. Look, I . . ."

The operator cut in demanding money.

Quickly, Moser told her where to find maps, instructions, forged paperwork—in the saddlebags on his Harley, along with his apartment key. *Piece of cake* was the last thing she heard before the call cut off. It dawned on her that because of love or the crime he had committed, or both, Moser might never come back.

Eleanor showered, dressed, went to work, stayed late. That night she crawled into bed with her headphones, reading light, pumpkin candle, herbal eye-pillow and sleeping pills, the exotic distractions of the lonely. Really, the bedside table looked like a sexual convalescent's.

Then she was asleep and the ape was on her again, this time lolloping down past her stomach with his warm, black, slick-honeyed tongue. Against her navel, she thought she heard an operatic vibration, a low hum. Stunned, she raised up on her elbows, looked around the empty room. She refused to get up and look in the garage, see if the latch was undone, if Hilton was where he was supposed to be. She had her suspicions and did not want the truth either way. Didn't happiness have a right to go unquestioned? And adult happiness, Eleanor knew, lasted longest when confined to tender arenas of ambiguity.

At the end of that night, Eleanor Stoddard changed the course of her life. She left an upbeat message on her manager's voice mail saying she quit, no hard feelings, she was now self-employed as a Living Barbie at little girls' birthday parties. And truthfully, before the inspection station, before the Strapless

Jock, Eleanor had done exactly that, thus her deceit was technical, her fib chronological. After investing in a slew of glittering costumes, she'd advertised that as Living Barbie she promoted a positive role model, teaching little girls that in modern-day America you could be both glamorous and successful. At the parties, the little girls were cold to her concept, whining and begging to try on her jewelry, bickering and tugging on her platinum wig with sticky, greedy fingers. Eleanor wound up putting an ad in the local alternative lifestyles newspaper and practically giving away her slinky wardrobe to a Presbyterian crossdresser. She finished the message by asking that somebody make certain Rorty got her Mr. Potato Head.

HILTON'S CAGE WAS jammed sideways in the backseat, the deep hem of a blue thermal blanket overhanging it like a limp awning. He was looking at her amorously, sucking water out of a pink jogger's bottle. The security guard floated in the passenger seat, stuffed into a sort of Brinks outfit and wearing reflective sunglasses. "Well boys," Eleanor rechecked Moser's maps, forged papers and instructions before switching on the ignition, "I don't know where the hell we're going, but here the hell we go." With that, she sped south out of Phoenix, down into Mexico and beyond. All doors and portals swung open, few questions were asked, hardly anyone stopped them. It was as if they possessed triune powers of invisibility, or more likely, the kind of visual absurdity that inspired long and cautious distance. Eleanor bit off her cartoon nails, gave away her spike heels and educational tapes. Glamour fell like confetti all along the way until she was barefoot, wearing a broomstick skirt and a *"Save the Rainforest"* T-shirt, her hair a little gray, though mostly still a flaming, hibiscus-color red.

She was spotted in Mexico City, Panama City, Managua and Bogotá, always with her clipping about the Cloud Chief, always asking directions. Before she vanished altogether, she was seen working in an orphanage, a soup kitchen, a General Motors plant, an AIDS clinic, a leper colony, behind the wheel of a lime-green taxi. Like a rogue saint, Eleanor Stoddard was sighted here and there, most often by the innocent, by the child working in a soybean field who said the lady gave him a message he couldn't remember, or the mute who signed he'd seen her in a diamond mine, a reading lamp blazing from her forehead. On occasion, she was seen in the company of a little ape. In bars and brothels, in certain classrooms and lunchrooms, there were heated debates and even fistfights over the whereabouts and purpose of the ape. The security guard? He went to the first listless knot of children she came across in Nogales, living like cockroaches in dank, poisonous sewers. They sold the toy for food, a slowly deflating joke to help them laugh.

Her image appeared on *retablos* made of tin or of wood, crude icons painted onto Coke bottles and votive candles. Redhaired, big-rumped piñatas swayed on poles in marketplace booths. She was a giantess on urban wall murals, cloud-skinned with snaking red hair, a banana-leaf hat, long feet. When rumor took hold that La Gringa had been abducted and murdered, bits of her flesh strung like superstition, like *milagros* around the necks of government soldiers, a second rumor sprang up to contradict the impossibility of the first—that she had found the Cloud People, and that their Chief, obedient to the riddle governing this lower world of dust and ash and insects, found strength to take La Gringa for his bride. Those of a melancholic temperament clung to the first rumor, while those with faith in the brutality of love defected, with fever, to the second.